Ebony chronicles of ELEVATION
VOLUME 1

An NCM Production

Published by NCM Publishing

All rights reserved. Without limiting the rights under copyright reserved above. No part of this book may be reproduced, stored in or introduced into a retrieval system, or transmitted, in any form, or by any means (electronic, mechanical, photocopying, recording, or otherwise), without prior written consent from both the author, and publisher NCM Publishing, except brief quotes used in reviews. For information regarding special discounts or bulk purchases, please contact NCM Publishing at orders@ncmpublishing.com

PUBLISHER'S NOTE:

This book is a work of fiction. Names, Characters, Places, and incidents either are products of the author's imagination or are used fictitiously. Any resemblance to actual events or locales or persons, living or dead, is pure and entirely coincidental.

Copyright © 2011 by NCM Publishing
All Rights Reserved, including the right of reproduction in whole or in part of any form.
ISBN **978-0983346166**
Library of Congress Catalog Card Number: 2011941048

Ebony Chronicles of Elevation
Written by: Various Authors
Edited by: David Good, The Editing One, Moses Miller
Text Formation: Write On Promotions
Cover Design and Layout: Donnie Ramsey

COPYRIGHT NOTICES

"A Black Man's Voice"
Copyright © By Omar Tyree

"Decisions"
Copyright © 2011 by Corey Barnes

"Broke in Cycles"
Copyright © 2011 by Moses Miller

"Facebook Friends"
Copyright © by Q. B. Wells

"Down Fall"
Copyright © by Eyone Williams

"My Heart"
Copyright © by Chris Hicks

"Willowbrook"
Copyright © by Norris Pimpton

CONTENTS

INTRODUCTION
A Black Man's Voice
Omar Tyree

Decisions
Corey Barnes

Broke in Cycles
Moses Miller

Facebook Friends
Q. B. Wells

Down Fall
Eyone Williams

My Heart
Chris Hicks

Willowbrook
Norris Pimpton

The Black Man's Voice/A Foreword

Omar Tyree

Since the jump off of the new African-American writing and publishing renaissance of the recent 1990s, the voice, story, subject and readership of the material has been grossly dominated by black women. Leading with the legendary Terry McMillan and her groundbreaking third novel, Waiting to Exhale, *in 1992, the black world of publishing of the early, mid and late 1990s went BOOM, as strongly as the Harlem Renaissance era of the 1920s and 30s. However, instead of Zora Neal Hurston being one of the few and only women writers to add her voice and a female perspective to the field of literature in the 1920s and 30s, this time around the black woman's voice and story has been the lead focus.*

With Terry McMillan, Toni Morrison, Alice Walker, BeBe More Campbell, Rosalyn McMillian, Octavia Butler, April Sinclair, Sheneska Jackson, Barbara Neely, J. California Cooper, Tina McElroy Ansa, Marita Golden, Gloria Naylor, Donna Hill, Mary Monroe, Lolita Files, Diane McKinney-Whetstone, Benilde Little, Kimberly Lawson Roby, Teri Woods, Vickie Stringer, Zane, Mary Marrison, Sister Souljah, Nicola Mitchell, and even British sister Zadie Smith, the game has been overrun with the sister story of every types. And the names above are not even *half* of the women authors who have contributed.

Then you have the men, with celebrated mystery writer Walter Mosley leading the charge, followed by E. Lynn Harris, Eric Jerome Dickey, Michael Baisden, Stephen Barnes, R.M. Jackson, Colson Whitehead, Trey Ellis, Shannon Holmes, Kwan, J.L. King, Carl Weber, and myself.

And ironically, despite all of the women who continue to dominate the black publishing game, the "Big 4" of E. Lynn, Eric Jerome, Michael and myself, once ruled the industry for a short period during the late 90s, with Walter seemingly writing on his own internationally-accepted island.

Nevertheless, where politics, manhood and race matters were the prime subjects and focus of the Harlem Renaissance era men, the new renaissance era men were forced to write more about relationships and matters of the heart, subjects of which a more female-based readership could relate to. Hence, the presence of the strong black male voice has been lacking. Not that there haven't been efforts to present the strong black male voice in this new literary era, they just haven't been well received. Their thunderous drums have been drowned out by the blaring horns of the sister stories.

Funny how things have changed and flipped around from Zora to Terry. Regardless, there remains a dire NEED for gender balance in the African-American community of contemporary literature. How can a black woman claim to understand the black man, whom she spends so much time trying to adapt to, appease, cohabitate with, and raise families and children with, if she cannot or will not understand his important perspectives on life? Granted to say, the largest section of African-American female-content has included the black man shaking, quaking, taking and breaking her heart. And what has he had to say for himself in his own words? . . . Nothing!

With that immanent need for the black man's perspective in mind, over the past five years of my career, I have penned three novels and two short story books, including; *What They Want, The Last Street Novel, Pecking*

Order, *Dirty Old Men* and *12 Brown Boys*, all to highlight the struggles and issues of contemporary African-American brothers from young to old.

This following collection of desperately needed black male voices from new writers continues the work of my mission, which is to add the willing artistic, intellectual and soul foul dance partners to the mix of hundreds of black women writers, who have been writing and dancing solo. So I was indeed thrilled to help compile, produce, organize and edit the following brothers, who continue to write with courage and purpose, a clear understanding of their concerns and struggles in the 21st Century. And I honor and celebrate them for doing so.

Sincerely,

Omar Tyree

An award-winning, *New York Times* bestselling author @ www.OmarTyree.com

Decisions

Corey J. Barnes

Chapter 1
Zeno

"All I got is $20. Let me get some of that butt naked."

"Man, you know that butt naked starts at $50. For $20, you can get some of this ye yo, or two dime sacs. Otherwise, you trippin."

I knew his name. It was Willie. But I called him man on purpose. Using names made things personal. In this game, you didn't want anything personal. That shit would get you in trouble at some point, so I stayed away from that.

"Please, just this time Zeno. I promise I will come correct next time."

As I looked at this shell of a man, a man who used to own his own dry cleaning business up off of MLK, I almost threw up my dinner. Something about the whole scene, remembering how he lost his business in a fire and had no insurance to cover it made me feel sorry for him. His wife left him and took their daughter and moved out of state. He lost everything. So much so that I went ahead and gave him what he wanted.

I gave him that dream killer.

Ebony Chronicles of Elevation

Hell, if he didn't spend his money here, he would just go around the corner to another block and spend it there. Might as well get it here and get what he wanted.

"Don't come back around here unless you got your money right. No more freebies. I mean that shit!"

"Okay Zeno, I promise…"

And off he went. I watched him scurry back into his little hole like a common house rat to smoke himself one step closer to heaven or hell.

Looking at Willie had soured my mood for the evening, so I packed up my stuff and began to head home about an hour before I planned to.

I hated being out here on this damn corner. It had been over four years since I had to be out here. Actually, I wouldn't even be out here right now if it wasn't for people like Willie. I had to get rid of two of my workers who had this block because word got back to me that they were giving out freebies and skimming off the top from me. Had the nerve to be out here with their own thing on the side, on my block!

I had seven blocks, seven groups working them and they reported to me on alternating days on a weekly basis. I had anywhere from two to five people working each block, never more than that because it brought too much attention, too much heat. Their day to check in was Wednesday. I found out about their side hustle from my first lieutenant, who got the Intel from his chick who lived over that way. So I got with him and we both rolled up on them a couple of days early, on Sunday as soon as I left church and had dropped my son off with his babysitter. Had my three piece suit on with matching gators and all, we caught them fools red handed!

At this point, I had a decision to make. It was either kill them or let them go from my employ. I never understood why they tried me like that. I paid them well, kept them protected, the best of both worlds. But you live long enough and nothing surprises you.

They must have caught me on a good day because I let them live, but not before I made them hurt and bleed. I figured bleeding and breathing that they could be mouth pieces for anybody else who thought about trying me like that. It had been a week and I still had not got my new workers yet, so I had to do the work myself. I couldn't have the block unattended because you never knew when some new jack was waiting to try and take the crown.

There was always somebody ready to take the crown. It was the nature of the business I was in. Of the life I led.

I have been at this racket, running these streets and this side of town for eight years now. From my first night making that run with my cousin to now being the HNIC, I had made this into a six figure a year business.

And I hated every minute of it.

Chapter 2

Zeno

My name is Raphael Thomas. In the streets I go by Zeno. Every day I wake up, I ask myself how I ended up like

Ebony Chronicles of Elevation

this. By this time, I was supposed to be playing pro ball for the San Francisco 49ers, throwing TD passes to Terrell Owens or Michael Crabtree, Vernon Davis, somebody. Suppose to be on the California coast with my wife, two kids, and the white picket fence that signifies that you have made it.

I was an all star quarterback coming out of high school and had a full athletic scholarship to play football at Florida State University. I was recruited by the legendary Bobby Bowden himself. Came and sat right in my living room on the couch and talked to my grandmother about how he would take care of me and make sure I was safe down in Tallahassee. My grandmother trusted him and that was all it took for me. In the fall, I was scheduled to leave Atlanta and head down to Florida and begin my career.

One night during my senior year, in an all star game no less. I was going in for the game winning touchdown, made a cut one way, my knee went the other, and by the time I awakened from the pain killers in the hospital bed, the doctor told me my knee was shattered and my football career was over. Around the same time, I found out that this hood rat I got with one night at a party was pregnant. Of course, I fought it. Asked for DNA test and all. And just like an episode of Maury, the test results came back and said I was the father!

So now I had a baby on the way, my lifelong dream smashed (no pun intended) at the young age of 18 and no job or plan on how I was going to take care of my child. One night, my cousin Larry asked me to go make a run with him. Told me all I had to do was be a look out, didn't have to touch or do anything. He said his normal partner had gotten himself in trouble at home with his dad. He had heard that he was doing some illegal stuff and wouldn't let him go. I went, against my better judgment and it was actually pretty easy. I just stood on a porch of an empty house watching the cars and people pass by. I had a cell phone Larry gave me that I was to text him 911 if I saw anything that didn't look right. Once the job was done, I went with him to settle up with the local kingpin at the time Maxie. When I walked in with Larry, he immediately slapped the taste out of my cousin's mouth and pointed a 9 MM directly at my temple. He asked Larry how he dare bring somebody new in on his shit without clearing it with him first. Larry tried to tell him that his normal partner couldn't go and he couldn't do it alone. Maxie didn't interrupt, so Larry continued and told him that I was his cousin and the only reason he asked me to go is because I was the only person he could trust. So Maxie turned around and asked me if I was trustworthy.

He still had that cannon up to my head. I had never been so scared in all of my life but I figured that showing fear or weakness right now wouldn't be smart. So instead of crying like a bitch like I wanted to, I looked him dead in the eye like a man, didn't flinch or blink, and said "Yeah I am."

Maxie stood about 6'1" and weighed about 200 pounds. I was 6'3" and 215 and was well put together. Growing up in the projects like I did, you didn't have time to be scared of nothing or nobody. I hadn't backed down from anything and it had served me well. Apparently, Maxie believed so also, as he took down his 9, smiled at me with a mouth full of gold teeth, and said "I like you, you got heart. I can use you on my team. What's your name?"

Relieved to have that thing out of my face, my first instinct was to knock his ass the fuck out. I was sure I could whoop his ass if it was straight up and fair. But the ten or so guys around him told me that it would be anything but that, so I let it go and said "Raphael".

Shaking his head and stroking his goatee, he said "Naw, a lil G like you needs another name besides Raphael. Something that the streets will respect. From now on, your name is Zeno. Yeah, I like that..."

He chuckled and the rest of his entourage did as well. I guess it was official. That was eight years ago, when Raphael died and Zeno was born.

The start of my story, my legend, my empire...

Chapter 3

Zeno

Another day in the ATL.

I woke up and went over to my window, pulled back the curtains and let the sun shine in.

"Let there be light!" I playfully exclaimed as I beat my chest like Tarzan. I lived way out in the suburbs of Stone Mountain. That was on purpose. I didn't want to live anywhere near where I did my dirt. If I had to, if it was just me, I wouldn't mind it at all, but I had another reason for my place of residence.

R.J.

Almost on cue, my slightly cracked door burst open and in rushed the ball of energy that was my son and jumped on my bed and onto my back before I had a chance to react.

"Daddy! Daddy! What are you doing?"

I checked to myself and a big smile spread across my face as I answered the joy of my life and said, "Just soaking in the sunshine."

"Do I have to go to school today? I don't feel so good."

I shook my head and said, "Yes you do. How are you going to be the next Barack Obama without an education? And by the way, wasn't you sick just yesterday too? Remember, no school, no practice."

Almost instantly, my son straightened up and said he was okay and sped out as quickly as he came in, saying he loved me. He always made my heart melt with that one. Why his mom could get herself strung out on drugs and make herself unfit to care for her child is still a mystery to me. Three year ago, I assumed full custody of my son and he hasn't seen her since. RJ was a very good football player. Actually a lot better than me, or at least I hoped so. He loved football and I never missed a practice or a game since he started playing. This was so much different from where I grew up, from where I made things happen now it wasn't funny. I wanted my son as far away from that world as possible.

He went to private school and Consuelo, my live in nanny, took real good care of him. I had one of my sergeants assigned to them both 24/7. They never knew he was around but he always was. Couldn't never be too sure and when it came to my son, I wasn't. I bought this house the same time I bought the one in Tampa as proof to myself that there was life after all of this. Life after this hell I was living in on Earth now.

Chapter 4

Zeno

When Maxie went down, he was over five blocks down in South Atlanta. Being the first lieutenant at the time, his right hand man, I was next in line to the throne. I had expanded our control to seven blocks, from Camp Creek to Greebriar, all the way over to Campbellton. I ran it all.

"Zeno, man what you gonna do about them privates over on Campbellton? Word is they bringing heat to the spot."

My first sergeant Hank didn't like the three workers I had over there and he didn't try to hide it.

"I don't think they nothing to worry about. You need to let it go with them cats. You still just mad that Lil Tony knocked up your little sister."

All of the rest of guys in the house burst out laughing, which surprised me because I didn't mean it as a joke. Hank didn't think it was funny either and clenched his fists like he wanted to fight. He knew better than to try me, so he turned his attention toward one of the other guys, rushed him and was to about take off on him until I told him to stop. While all of this was going on, the house phone rang, which meant only one thing, somebody was calling from the county jail collect. You couldn't call cell phones collect and the number was only given out to a couple of my soldiers that got locked up. Usually, I answered, called their chick or their mom on three-way and put it down for the fifteen minutes allotted time for the call. I picked up and heard the customary *you have a collect call from the Dekalb County Jail, will you accept the charges?* I said yes and then was surprised by the voice on the other end.

"What's up Zeno?"

I almost dropped the phone from surprise. It had been over two years since I heard Maxie's voice. I used to go see him faithfully, but had stopped when he told me not to come back, to hold it down like he taught me and not worry about him anymore.

"What's going on Maxie? Been a long time."

"I know, I know. Got your number from your cousin Larry in here a couple of weeks ago. I just decided to call now though. How's everything going?"

I was at a loss for why he would be calling out of the blue like this, so I figured I would wait to hear what he had to say first.

"Everything good, no complain'ts Maxie. How you doing in there?"

"Things fine in here, just nothing but time and walls, nothing but time and walls. Had an interesting conversation the other day with a couple of guys in here. You wanna know what we talked about Zeno?"

Scratching my head and squinting my eyes, I answered back, "Naw what?"

I heard a loud sigh on the other end of the phone and then he replied "Snitching."

One thing you never wanted your name associated with on the street was being a snitch. It was like a death warrant.

"Really, wow that's sounds interesting."

"Yeah I thought so. All this time, all these years, I thought that the feds just caught me, that my luck had run out. But now some of these lil niggas in here are saying that I got set up. Saying I had a snitch in my army, a mole in the organization. So although I haven't talked to you in a while, I just called to give you some two cent advice to take it or trash it."

"And what's that Maxie."

A long stint of silence on the other end ensued. Then he said "Watch your back". Before I had a chance to answer, I heard a click.

And a dial tone. And me holding the phone wondering what the hell that call was all about.

Chapter 5

Zeno

Dreams.

We all have them.

I remember an old Martin Lawrence episode where the character, bruh man, talked about "Freud nem" saying that dreams were really repressed desires of what we really wanted. I wondered if that just applied to dreams you had when you were sleep, because I had been daydreaming like crazy lately. Daydreams and thoughts that took me far away from here: I couldn't sell dope all of my life. At some point, I had to move on. I didn't consider myself the normal drug dealer. I didn't have a mouth of gold teeth, didn't wear a lot of flashy jewelry, didn't walk around with wads of cash in my pocket, didn't have a tricked out car with crazy paint job and big rims, with loud music blasting out of it. I wore my pant above my waist and wore a belt. Lastly, I didn't carry a gun.

Now there were plenty of dudes on my team and especially in my special army that did. That was the nature of the game. It said you had to stay strapped, or be around people who did and didn't mind using it if it came down to it. I hated stereotypes; the streets were full of them. I actually owned two houses and had at least three bank accounts. But to stay two steps ahead of the game, I had all of it in my grandmother's name. It would be impossible for me to try and explain how I got all of this with no job. In this way, the feds couldn't touch it if it came down to it. Had two life insurance policies, one with my grandmother as the beneficiary and the other with my son getting it all.

Half a mil each.

Gotta be real about this thang. It's tough out here in these streets and any day could be your last if it was your time to go. I even had a will. Like I said, I am not your normal pharmaceutical engineer.

Ebony Chronicles of Elevation

My daydreams took me down to sunny Florida, opening up my very own combination barber shop and tax office. I love working with numbers and money, I picked up an online tax certificate from a class I took a few years back. That's how I flip my money so good. I got into stocks the same time I got that tax license. You can buy, sell, and trade and never even leave the house. Cutting hair is my hobby. I fade all my team up for free for the practice. Have gotten real good at it if I do say so myself. Just gave my son a Mohawk last week and he says all the kids at school say he is so "cool" with it.

Yeah, I could really see myself living that life, just me, my son, and my grandma. I had enough saved up that I could walk away from this today and not look back.

EVER.

As I sat and wrestled with my thoughts, really contemplating making them reality for the first time, the door swung open and in burst one of my sergeants, Charlie, out of breath and hysterical.

"Zeno, Zeno man these young fools out here trippin!"

I stood up and walked over to my man and got him to calm down because I couldn't understand half of what he was saying.

"Calm down Charlie, sit back, relax, and slowly tell me what's going on."

I had one of the guys bring him some water and I waited for him to drink up before he spoke again.

"Alright Zeno, I'm good now. There is this young cat named Xay that say he trying to come see about you over on Grenbriar. Say you done ran that block long enough and it is time to break bread or move out the way."

Now while I was ready to put this thing down, to let it go, to walk away, I would. But I would do it when I felt like it and I would be damned if some lil young come up was gonna force me out and take what's mine. Call it foolish pride. It's a man thing I guess but this lil punk had just tried my G.

"Oh really, is that right?" I said while stroking my goatee. My adrenaline immediately started flowing like I was about to play a football game. I started to rub my hands together quickly, the universal sign that meant it was about to go down and said, "Where that cat get it down at?"

These younguns ain't got no respect. Guess they gotta be taught some.

"Alright, lets squad up!"

I hadn't had to call a squad up in over two years. That was the last time some new jack tried me. That time it was over on Camp Creek. That war got kind of messy, I lost a couple of my best soldiers in that one, but cemented my legend with how I went and took out all four of them cats. I did that in one sweep, true gangsta style. I made sure that all their funeral arrangements were taken care of, even set up college funds for the three kids if they ended up going. I hope this didn't have to get that bad. Those guys just didn't want to listen, compromise, or nothing. I really had no choice. I really hoped me and this Xay guy could sit down, talk like men, and come to an understanding. That's what I hoped but my gut told me otherwise. My man Charlie didn't flinch much. If he was this upset, it was with good reason. Besides him, my lieutenant Amp was the only other one on my team I trusted fully with everything. If he said they were trippin, then they were. It meant he had already tried to work something out. Coming to me meant it hadn't worked. That's the problem when you have a rational person dealing with an irrational one. Been a long time since I had to bring the pain, but it looked like it might be that time again.

Chapter 6

Zeno

I found out the cat Xay had one team, about eight strong. I didn't know how trigger happy they were, so I decided to hold back with the squad up for now, which really disappointed some of my guys. They lived for that type of party, but not me. I got his phone number from one of the lil chicks he messed with and decided to call him first and set up a meet and greet, or at least try to.

He picked up on the 3rd ring. I called him from a pre-paid phone. The same one I made all my deals and connects with the Italians on, totally untraceable.

"Who is this?"

These young folks ain't got no manners I thought to myself while shaking my head.

I calmly replied, "Xay, this is Zeno. I think the time has come for us to talk."

"Man, what the fuck we need to talk about?"

It was very important that one of us remain calm right now or this could quickly go the wrong way. Since he was already cursing, it seemed that person was gonna have to be me.

"Now Xay, there is no need for the language. If you are gonna be in the game, you gotta be a man about yours. Emotions can get you in trouble if you don't control them."

I didn't want to have to go in and do a Scarface or Sugar Hill to prove a point, but I would if pressed on it. After a brief pause, he replied, "What you talking about?"

I smiled on my end of the phone. I had the gift of gab. I could talk an Eskimo into buying some ice. So I felt good when he asked that and said, "Lets meet over at Ultimate Bar and Grill on Camp Creek, you know the place? We can eat, drink, and talk about things."

Say 6 pm, about an hour from now."

I knew that Ultimate had uniformed police officers in the parking lot and security patted you down coming in, so I figured that I wouldn't have to worry about any gun play and we could focus on the business at hand.

I arrived at Ultimate by 5:30. I hated being late to anything, hated people who did. In the dope game, being late could get you killed. I picked a table in the back and sat where I could see the entire room and all of the doors. Couldn't have any surprises, at any time.

Promptly at 6:00, in walked who I assumed to be Xay. He had the textbook and stereotyped drug dealer swag going. He walked over to me and had two dudes with him, all three of them mean mugging me. I chuckled aloud as they made their way to the table.

"Thanks for coming again, Xay. No need for the hostility. I already ordered some wings and fries. They got the best lemon pepper wings in all of Atlanta in here. I didn't know what you were sipping on, so I didn't order. Also, this meeting is just between me and you, so you can tell your men to go hang out at the bar or something, we just gonna talk."

I figured he would not come alone. Didn't get to where I was by not always being on my game. I had my lieutenant and my other sergeant besides Charlie two tables over in deep cover mode. Since they already knew Charlie by face, he had to sit this one out. The Ultimate people patted you down but didn't check your shoes, especially inside boots. Both of my men had a little something inside just in case. With younguns, you really never knew. Better safe than sorry.

The Xay guy looked to be in his early twenties, a little under my age. He was about 5'10" and about 185 pounds, put you in the mind that dude that played O Dog in the movie Menace to Society. He sat down at the table, still trying to look hard and play the role. While he did that, I ate a wing dripped in ranch dressing and called the waitress over to the table. He ordered a beer and I got water. I never drank when doing business. I needed to be able to think straight. Everything I was trying not to do with my look and style, this guy Xay openly flaunted. He would fit on the front cover of Dope Boy magazine or Feds Look at Me Illustrated, if there was such a thing.

"So Xay, thanks again for coming. I really only have one question: What makes you think you should be able to have Greenbriar when I have been running it for years?"

Before he could answer, the fine waitress had come back with his beer and my water, so he paused before speaking. Once she left, he did.

"It's really simple, you been running it for years but it has only been on loan to you. And the loan period is about up."

I was now both intrigued and confused at the same time but instead of talking I kept quiet and let him continue talking.

"You see, I am just the messenger sent to reclaim my family's property."

"Family's property?" I blurted out before I had a chance to catch myself and totally going against my original plan.

Sitting up in the chair, he took a swig of his beer and replied "Yeah my family. Before you were on this block, my uncle ran this block. You know my uncle, Maxie. Well he is coming home soon and he's coming for what's his and he's coming to see about you too."

My head was now spinning with this information this guy Xay had just spit. He claimed to be Maxie's nephew and said he was coming to get his turf back and coming for me. I was lost but managed a confused "Coming for me for what??"

Xay took one of the wings, sucked the meat right off down to the bone and threw it on the plate. Wiped his hands and mouth and said, "Yeah he say he coming for you. Word on the street is that you set my uncle up. There were a couple of niccas that wanted to do you when it came out but my uncle said no. Said to leave you be and let you breathe. That he gonna see about you personally when he get out."

I almost dropped my water when he said that. I stood up out of my seat and said "What you trying to say? I'm a snitch?!?! Man I should kick your lil ass for bringing that bullshit my way. I ain't never been no damn snitch, don't even try me like that."

The roles had reversed. Xay was now the calm one and I was the one showing emotion. He seemed to enjoy this as he was chuckling and smiling broadly now. He stood up to leave and said, "Like I said, that's what the streets say and what my Uncle say. He just asked me to get word to you that he is on the way."

And with that, he took one more wing, drank the last of his beer, motioned to his two men and left the bar, leaving me there to stew in my juices and digest what he had just said.

Chapter 7

Zeno

A snitch.

The lowest form of a person.

Like a rat or something on the bottom of your shoe.

I had been called a lot of things in my day, but never a snitch. Dudes got took out on the daily for turning state on a nicca. I had called it in on a couple myself since I became the King. At the end of the day, all a man got is his reputation. He loses that, he might as well get out the game quick. That lil nigga callin me a snitch had me all messed up. I took shit like that personal. I hadn't said a word about it or the conversation the whole ride to the house. I just stared out the window at the cars passing by.

"Zeno, man what that lil nicca had to say?"

That was Nate Dogg, my right hand man. Nate was usually quiet by nature but had been with me long enough to know that when I got quiet, something was on my mind.

I turned toward him and got eye contact with him in the rearview and answered, "Nothing baby. I'm cool."

He made a loud gruff type sound and didn't say anything else. Nate was a big man. I mean a really big man, like 6'5" and close to 300 pounds. I hired him right from the security line at Strokers one night when we were heading in. I liked the way that nicca straight up beat down two fool who were cutting up in there without breaking a sweat. Made him an offer he couldn't refuse and he been riding with me every sense. I needed something to take my mind off that convo with Xay so I sat up in my seat and said to him "Nate, change of plans. Let's hit up Strokers. Everythings on me. Call up Charlie and tell him to meet us there."

I sat back in the seat and listened to the music as Nate turned the car around to go to our new destination.

Ebony Chronicles of Elevation

30 minutes later, we were pulling into the parking lot. Charlie was already out his car waiting for us at the door. As we walked up, I asked the security what the cover was and he said $20. I pulled out the money clip from my wallet and counted him off 5 doves and we all entered through the double doors. It had been awhile since I had been up in here. When I had a taste to see some ass now, I just had one of the guys set it up at the house. Nate still knew a lot of the girls so it wasn't real hard. Plus, I always made it worth their while.

I didn't really want to be at the house right now, needed to get my mind on other things. I liked what they had done with the place. It now had an open floor design, very nice sitting area to do your business you know. It was almost plush throughout. One thing I liked about this spot was that it was not too loud, no ghetto vibe at all. Some strip clubs in Atlanta, that was all they put out. Couldn't stand that. This place was almost tasteful, aside from the fact that ladies were shaking a little something for money. *Must be a couple of big spenders in here* I thought with all of the money I saw on the floor as we walked through. I liked upscale, top end stuff, even if I didn't come from it.

It looked like a patch of green field with all of the one dollar bills that lined the floor. I noticed how none of the dancers even made a move toward the money. They had their eyes on bigger fish it seemed. The kind who didn't even touch one dollar bills any more. It almost seemed a little like a competition. This was why I kept my business private and at the house. No lines, no waiting, pick of the lot if I wanted it.

About three lap dances and a couple of drinks later, I was feeling pretty nice. I think Nate must have noticed because I caught him laughing at me out the corner of my eye.

"Man what's so damn funny?" I slurred my words toward him.

When I did that, he burst into full laughter, doubling over on the couch and all, almost causing the girl sitting on him to fall.

"I'm laughin at you man. I haven't seen you get on it in a good minute. I forgot how you be acting."

It had been awhile since I drank or smoked. Gave all that shit up when my son's delivery system brought him into the world. I saw what that shit did to her. Saw what it did to people every day. I took one look at my son in my arms as a baby and stopped all that shit cold turkey. Never looked back either. Tonight was the first time in a very long time.

Clearing his throat and sitting up on the couch, Nate continued "Seriously though, I figured you drinking and up in here because of what that young cat said to you. Now are you gonna tell me what he said or am I gonna have to keep asking you."

I looked over at Nate and saw he wasn't going to let it go. I took a sip from my cup, put it down and answered his question.

"Man, that lil nicca called me a snitch. Said that Maxie is his uncle and that he was coming to see about me personally when he got out in a lil bit. That the reason I hadn't been touched already was because he gave the word from the inside not to. Man, I might be a lot of things, but I ain't no damn snitch. That shit got me all fucked up in the head."

Nate was an old school G. He was about ten years or so older than me. He didn't do a lot of talking, sat back and watched things and see how it went. He didn't say nothing for like five minutes. Then he spoke, slow and low, saying "Man, why you letting that shit stress you? You know you ain't no snitch. I know you ain't no snitch. That's all that matters. I wonder why Maxie think that though. We gotta see whats up with that."

Nate was like an old uncle to me. When he talked, he always spoke saying we, never I. He was a soldier, but always family.

"So that means the streets think I am some kind of damn snitch. All I got is my rep Nate. I can't have these fools out here thinking I am the feds. I might as well pack it up and go home."

"Zeno, look here man. Don't worry about your rep or these streets. Ain't nobody comin at you, they ain't that crazy. I wanna know what fool trying to put salt in the game by lying on you like that?"

That was something I wanted to know as well. It could have been them cats I ran off the block a lil while back. Or maybe them clowns from a few years back that tried to run up before they had to see what time it was. For the most part, nobody tried me and I didn't come across sideways to nobody either. I liked to stay off the radar, as hands off as possible. But now, it seemed like that was out the window.

Nate broke up my train of thought by saying, "Instead of trying to figure this shit out on your own, won't you just go to the source. Go see Maxie and see what he got to say."

Nate was right. He usually was when he spoke. I could sit around and try to figure this shit out on my own. Go through everybody that I had beef with and be here all night. Or I could just ride to Fulton County Correctional and get it straight from the horse's mouth. Really, that was the only thing to do. I knew it. Nate knew it, wasn't hard to figure out. I took one last drink from my cup and told Nate it was time for us to go. I needed to get home and sleep this liquor off tonight. Tomorrow, I had a ride to make to get some answers.

Chapter 8

Zeno

"Yeah, that wasn't how that was supposed to go down. My nephew can get a little overly aggressive at times. I have had to speak to him about that a time or two. I apologize to you for him jumping the gun like that. That conversation was supposed to be between me and you, face to face when I got out."

One thing Maxie had always been was direct and to the point. You never had to worry or wonder where you stood with him. So the way I took it he had his nephew on standby and he couldn't wait. Big uncle had to reprimand him for it.

"You know Zeno, you have to give what you want in return. When I was out and was the king, I always handled people with respect, no matter what. I only had to personally take out two guys in my time in the streets and that was in self defense. I am very proud of that. I like to think that it had a lot to do with the way I treated people. I was always straight up and above all else honest."

I let the man who taught me everything about the game that I knew and did not interrupt. Part of the respect thing he was going over with me right now. Knowing him like I did, he would be coming right out with whatever it was he wanted to say face to face to me real soon. So I just listened and waited for it.

"Next month will be eight years I been in this cage. When that judge said 96 months back then, I didn't even allow myself to begin to try and count the days. I have read and seen where cats have gotten out of here for good behavior after only doing half the time. Around here you know what good behavior means Zeno? It means you turned state and working with the feds."

He was looking right at me when he made that last comment. Eye to eye. He didn't blink. Neither did I.

"Guess that is why they made me do all 96 months. But next month, they gotta let me go. They can't hold me no more. They came at me a couple of times about giving them information to reduce my time. But my bid said 96, so I was prepared to do 96. While you in here, you have a chance to hear things and pick up stuff. You know what I mean Zeno?"

He knew I didn't. I hadn't ever been locked up, so how could I?

Chuckling lightly, he said "Of course not. I picked up a college degree since I been in here. Got me a degree in Business Administration. Figured I would need that when I get out to make my money work for me. Picked up the Koran like Denzel did in that movie and became a Muslim. Don't eat pork no more, none of that. Right here in this cage, I also heard how I got put here. How I was set up."

Now we were getting somewhere. Now we were getting to the point of the drive up here. I clasped both of hands together and let my chin rest on them and let Maxie continue talking.

"When I first got in here, all I could think about was that night and how the police was there. They told me that the deal I made was to an undercover, but there was never one who took the stand in my trial. I had made the same deal twenty times over and never had a problem. Pre-paid cell phones. Out of state rental cars. Remote locations. The blueprint to years of success. It was fool proof. As soon as I opened the briefcase, they came in from everywhere, even knew all the escape routes up in there. They got me, my two lieutenants, and the Italians we had the deal set up with. Now I had my people to check, and everybody who was there that night did his full bid. That let me know it wasn't none of them. I almost just chalked it up to bad luck and my time finally coming. If you stay in this game long enough, every man time eventually come."

Once again he paused. Once again he looked at me eye to eye. Once again, he didn't blink, and neither did I.

He continued.

"One day while out in the yard, I was under the weight bench and young blood walks up on me and says it was a shame how I got set up like that. Just out the blue. When I first looked at him, I didn't recognize him, but when I looked closer I did. He had changed his appearance, but you can't change your eyes. I still remembered his eyes from when we were both on the outside. I told him that was some heavy stuff to say if he couldn't back it up. He told me could, so I listened. I listened as he told me how it was only one guy who stood to gain from me going down. Only one guy who didn't hit that was one of my officers in the whole thing. One person who kept his nose clean through the whole thing. That was you Zeno."

I now took the chance to speak because I had heard enough.

"Maxie, so you are saying that this random guy just rolled up on you in here and told you that I dimed you out? How much sense does that make? You are a smart man, I mean really, how much sense does that really make?"

Maxie stood up from the chair and walked over toward the door and looked through the window. Then he answered.

"That was the same thing I was thinking Zeno. But then, this guy is in here. I looked up his bid and he got longer than I do. I got to thinking, how is that everybody went down but you?"

I interrupted him and said, "because I wasn't there Maxie. You remember you wouldn't let me go. You told me I wasn't ready. So I sat at the spot and waited for you guys to get back. Man I never wanted to be this deep in the game. You knew that. We talked about it. I never wanted to be the king. Hell, at the time they got you, I was like #4 or #5 on the list. When all of ya'll went down, I was the only one left.

If I was trying to set ya'll up, why would I have even asked to go?"

Maxie stopped and looked kind of confused for a minute before speaking again.

"Zeno, I loved you like a son. I still do. The truth of the matter is. It doesn't really matter at this point. The bottom line is that there can't be two kings. The streets are not built for it. In a month, you have a choice to make, move out the way or get pushed out of the way. Either way, I gotta come get what's mine."

Before I had a chance to answer, he called for the guard to open the door and for him to go back the cage he had lived in for the past 95 months. He took one look back through now tear filled eyes and left without anymore words spoken. Left me there speechless and with a lot to think about.

Chapter 9

Zeno

The scoreboard read 21-17. We were losing the game but we were driving. I was positioning my team for the winning touchdown and the national championship at Florida State University. I was barely able to hear myself think in the Superdome it was so loud. The Ohio State Buckeyes were the number 1 team in the land and every expert had picked them to win this game. Said we didn't have a chance and that next year would be our year. I wasn't even supposed to be playing. Next year was going to be my year. I was just the backup, calling in the plays through my clipboard. Then the 2nd quarter, our starting senior quarterback went down with a knee injury, coach called my number and here I was. As the seconds ticked down off the clock, I called the final play. I brought my team up the line, took the snap, dropped back to pass, saw a receiver breaking free in the back of the end zone, let it fly and......

"Sorry for waking you Senor Raphael, you have a phone call and the person on the other line says that it is urgent!!"

I turned over in my bed to seen Consuelo looking at me through big brown eyes. I guess I must have been dreaming.

Ugh.

Not an ugh because I was awakened, but more so an ugh because of the dream I was awakened from. That was the game I was supposed to be playing in and in charge of, not this one. I had grown very weary of this one as of late. After that trip to see Maxie, Florida is looking better and better all the time.

"Where is the phone?"

"Here you go sir," she replied handing it too me.

Turning my attention to the phone, I answered, "Hello?"

A low voice came through the phone on the other end, saying "We need to talk."

I checked for eye boogers and seeing none I rolled over to sit up on the side of the bed, slid on my bedroom shoes and stood up and walked over to the window.

"Right now, man? I was getting a good nap in."

"Yeah man, right now. I think we have a leak, we may have been infiltrated."

Damn, that was some heavy shit to be insinuating. I knew my right hand knew this and he would not even bring that kind of mess to me if it didn't have some truth to it. Another thing he and everybody else in my crew knew was when I was with my son, that I was off limits. Usually, I was on call but this time for me was sacred.

I looked over on the other side of the bed and saw my little man still asleep. We had just finished with an intense game of Michael Jackson on the Xbox Kinect and we were both wore out. I smiled when I thought about how he celebrated after he beat me. I didn't mind losing to him. Not at all. I went to the bathroom and splashed some water on my face to gain some focus. When I moved out here, it went against everything society said was wrong with black people. Get some money, move out the neighborhood. Get some money, go and buy a Mercedes Benz. Get some money, go get you a white girl. One out of three ain't bad I guess.

I called Consuelo back into the room and asked her to watch my son while I was gone out. I usually allowed her to leave early on Sundays off but I needed to make this run to see what was going on. I told her I would pay her double for staying. She told me that she was babysitting her grandson, so I told her that she could them drop him off here. I hated changing up her plans but she didn't seem to mind.

About 30 minutes later, I was in my Nissan Altima, the very first car I ever earned, the one I rode in when I wanted to stay low key, even after all these years, making my way to the spot. This thing was getting kind of serious and I needed to squash it as quickly as possible. If my man had a lead on where this lie had started, then I needed to get to the bottom of it ASAP and get things back to normal, or as close as it could be. After I took care of this, I could then focus all of my energy on this Maxie situation and what I was going to do about it.

Chapter 10

Maxie

I can't believe that these crackers gave me 8 years. And I can't believe they made me do all 96 months of this bid. I watched cats get cut loose with a whole lot more charges hanging on them than I had. This shit wasn't supposed to go down like this. I had the streets on lock. Went from just being on the streets to the king in less than two years. I thought I was untouchable. My set up was tight. No way I should have ever been caught. So when they kicked my door in, I took it all in stride as part of the game. At some point, everybody who is anybody in the game gets their door kicked in. I still was a little surprised though because I had all the cops that worked the neighborhood on my payroll and they basically looked the other way while I did my thing. The cat that kicked in my door was brand new. They transferred him up from Macon. He didn't know me from a can and pain't and damn sho didn't give a damn about me or my set up. He cuffed me and stuffed me like day old garbage.

My trial came up and everything was going fine at first. I had the best two lawyers money could buy. My own dream team. They were working that court room like Cochran, Darden, and that lawyer who got that white girl off who killed her baby in Florida. Poking holes in whatever the prosecution tried to stick me with. I could smell the fresh Atlanta air through my nostrils and a not guilty next to my name. But then, the hammer dropped.

They brought in my transaction book where I did all my book keeping with how much money I was bringing in. I didn't trust computers, so I still wrote my shit down. All of it. I had that thing locked up in my own safe in my floor in my house. I was the only one who knew that combination, so how did they get it? While I sat there trying to figure that shit out and my dream team not being able to explain that one away, they hit me with another body blow. They had recorded conversations of deals I had set up with my South Florida and Cuban connections, even had an informant that had infiltrated my army and moved his way up to sergeant. He got on the stand and talked about my set up, how deals were done, runs he had made when I had ordered guys to be taken out, step by step, play by play. I went from sugar to shit in a matter of a day. The jury deliberated for less than an hour before they came back with a guilty verdict for drug trafficking and three other charges. The judge gave me two years for each charge and ran them concurrently. My lawyers asked for leniency since I had never had so much as a traffic ticket but the judge wasn't hearing none of it. Eight years later, I am set to be released to that Atlanta air I thought I would get to smell eight years before.

A lot had changed since I went in. I went in with an afro and no facial hair and was coming out with a bald head and a goatee. I went in weighing a modest 185 lbs and was coming out a muscular 225. I went in as the king and was coming out as something other than that. Someone else had my throne. I would have been foolish to think that it wouldn't happen. Hell I got the throne after the guy before

Ebony Chronicles of Elevation

me went down, although he didn't go in, he got took out. But just the same, I came up after he went down. Such is life. Someone has to fall before someone else can rise. Sad but true. It is what it is.

I still remember the first time I met lil Zeno. He didn't want no parts of what his cousin had brought him in on. He had this whole vibe about him that said this was not for him at all. I still wonder if he had not gotten that girl pregnant would he have been there, or if he would not have gotten hurt playing ball. Although he didn't want to be there, he was a natural though. He was not a punk and wasn't scared of nothing or nobody. When I first went down, he was the only one who used to come and see me. I had grown to love that lil nigga like my son. He didn't want the throne. He told me that. I basically had to beg him to take it. I did so with the thought that I wouldn't have to do the whole bid in here and I could get out and take things back over. He would just be renting it in a sense. He seemed to be cool with that. Eight years later, he is the king, he done bought the house, stopped renting it a long time ago.

Now I was in between a rock and a hard place. I thought long and hard about giving the game up when I got out of here. I had enough money put away that I could chill and do fine for myself. I didn't have any family, no wife, no son, just me so it would be easy to just go somewhere and just chill. I know once I get out of here, I ain't doing nothing to come back. Can't spend another minute inside these walls. But once you have been the king, once you have been to the mountain top, a part of you will always want to go back. But I couldn't just go and say Hey Zeno, I am back, can I have these streets back? It didn't work that way.

He had a new army, the streets had changed, the game had changed. But I was still Maxie. And that meant something. My name still carried major weight. But like I said, Zeno was like my son, so I was really going both ways with how I was going to handle this thing. That is, until a month or so ago. I was at the table eating some of this mess they serve us up in here and a dude sat down across from me who looked familiar. He kept looking at me but wasn't saying nothing. Now I had been in here for eight years, but had not given up no ass or took no ass the whole time. I wasn't with that gay shit. I knew I was going to get out of here at some point and I wasn't coming out as no punk. I had nothing against gay people, I just wasn't one. I had to beat a couple of niggas down in here that tried me when I first got in and now nobody try me like that. So when this guy I didn't recognize kept sizing me up, I got ready for another beat down, which would probably add to my time before I got out, but I didn't care. Instead, he said "Maxie, you don't remember me?"

I squinted my eyes to see if I did, but I didn't. "Naw man, I don't know you. But you better stop looking at me like that before I give you what you looking for."

The guy started laughing and I felt myself getting mad. The other people must have felt it too because they begin to move out of the way.

Putting up both of his hands in front of him, the guy said "My bad Maxie, I didn't mean to laugh. But it's me Larry, from the block. Zeno's cousin. Don't beat my ass man, for real."

It was Larry. Damn, it had been forever since I seen him last and he looked like shit. He had a nappy afro and beard and looked like he was about 20 pounds lighter than when I saw him last. Looked like he had done went and gotten himself a drug habit. Damn.

Ebony Chronicles of Elevation

"Whats up Larry? Ain't seen you in a minute. What you in for?"

Dudes in here always asked that. I never understood why. I didn't give a damn while you were in, I was here to do my time and my time alone. But I had asked him the question I hated being asked.

"Man they got me for breaking and entering and burglary. Caught me coming out of a pawn shop with a bunch of shit. Third strike and shit."

We began to catch up on things. The neighborhood. How things were. Zeno. All that. In between, he said "Man it's fucked up how they set you up."

Now, for the seven and a half years I had been here, I had just told myself that I got caught. That somewhere I had slipped up, although I couldn't figure where or how. It just made it go better not to keep racking my brain about it. Now Larry was saying what I never allowed into my head and had my total interest and attention.

"What the fuck you mean how I got set up? What bullshit you talkin about?"

Larry looked like he had just realized he said something that he wasn't supposed to. Like he had told where the Christmas presents were hid the day before Christmas. He tried to back track and take it back, but it was too late.

"Man, it ain't my business Maxie. Don't make me say it. I don't want to be nowhere in it."

Agitated now, I replied, saying "Man you already in now. You better tell me what you know before I beat your ass down right now."

I hated to threaten him like that but I didn't have time to play with his ass.

"Well, you know how that informant who was an undercover had all that shit on you? Well, the word is that he was working with someone in your army that was helping him get all the shit he had on you."

"Somebody? Man who? I ain't got time to be trying to figure this shit out. Who nigga!!"

He dropped his head. He acted like he really didn't want to say anything, but didn't have a choice.

"Zeno."

I felt the breath leave my body for a minute and lost all focus. I know this fool didn't just say Zeno. The sam Zeno who I had grown to love like a son. The Zeno who I had the same cops who left me alone to do the same for him while I was in here. The Zeno who I gave the keys to the kingdom to. Hell naw, I wasn't believing that shit.

"Bitch stop lying."

"Maxie, I ain't lying. Ask yourself, how could that guy have gotten that close. Also ask yourself, who else had your code to your safe besides you. And before you say just you, remember one night you were drunk and gave the code to Zeno to make a run for you with the Italians. Word is, Zeno was tired of being the vice pres and ready to run things."

I sat down and digested all that he had just told me. My mind went to racing. The undercover had to have some help inside. It was no way I was slipping like that. And I did give Zeno my code, I had forgot all about that. No fucking way!! Zeno couldn't be the one. But all of the evidence pointed to him. Damn why did it have to play out like this? With this information, I had moved from in between the rock and the hard place and was now standing firmly on the rock. Zeno had turned me in.

Payback would be a bitch.

Starting tomorrow when I got out.

Chapter 11

Zeno

Sitting at the table at the spot was my man Jake and Craig. Three glasses all with Hennessey and Coke with ice cubes included in all. My man got straight to the point. I appreciated it, because at this point, I didn't have time for a long interlude and all of that.

"So, its like this....I got a partner who is doing a bid up at Fulton and he called me the other day. Said he overheard a conversation between Maxie and your cousin Larry."

I stopped sipping on my drink and looked over at Jake and repeated, "Larry? He in Fulton? I didn't even know that."

My man was like "Yeah, he caught a dope charge. Was up in Marietta trying to get his own thing going. They sent him back down here, and he met up with Maxie. My partner said that, basically Larry dimed you out. Told Maxie that you had done turned state when that undercover infiltrated and set him up. Said you were snitching and setting it all up so that you could get the throne. You felt it was your time to be the king."

I starred across the table at my man Craig. He stared back at me. Neither one of us blinked. It was like something straight out of a western movie.

"Craig, don't play with me man. I ain't in the mood for no bullshit. Straight up."

"Zeno, for real, would I play with you about something like this? Your cousin is in there lying on you man. That's why Maxie is so heated. Word is, he wanted the throne back but had no reason to come at you sideways since he gave it to you before he went in. Now this gives him a reason to go to war with you. But if he wants it, he can get it. I'll put it in his life straight up and down."

So, Craig went on to tell me that the story goes that Maxie been protecting me all the time he been in and the protection was off and he was coming for me because he thinks I set him up.

So there it was. The mystery solved. I hate being called a snitch by a snitch. Set up and hung out to dry by my cousin. My mother and his daddy were brother and sister. We grew up together in the same house and ate at the same table. Made us come up like brothers.

Larry done lied on me and was about to get a full-fledged street war off something that wasn't even true.

"So what is our plan of action Zeno? If these cats looking for a war, we can definitely bring it to them. All you gotta do is say the word and it is on."

I really couldn't focus on what Craig was saying. I was still back to the part about my first cousin lying on me. Why would he do that? What purpose did he have for throwing me to the wolves? One thing for sure, I could be a wolf to when I needed to be. Or a full grown dog. A bear. Insert the appropriate animal and I could be that. Hadn't had to be. Truth be told, really didn't like to. But it seemed that I would have to in this case. And that was perfectly fine with me. What I really wanted to do right now though was have a conversation with a certain cousin of mine. But it seemed that would have to wait. I had a counter attack to prepare for. This war it looked like inevitably was about to go down.

Chapter 12

Maxie

Man, I didn't know the sun shined this bright. Or the air smelled so good. Or something as simple as a traffic jam could be so nice to see. But all of the sights and sounds of Atlanta were a welcome sight for sore eyes. I had been gone for too long.

95 months, 12 days, 13 minutes of my life I gave to the Georgia Correctional System. We used to always talk on the yard how when we got out, we were going to do right. Get a regular job, make honest money. Give back and never come back in here. But everybody knows that is just talk.

Once a hustler, always a hustler. Code of the streets.

So when I got out here, the first thing I did was go and hit the old spots I used to run when I was on top. Everything had changed so much. I rode by the Amphitheater and saw that it had been remodeled. Went by Tri Cities High and word was now they were sorry as hell in football. They used to run things back in the day. I just shook my head at it all. Greenbriar Mall was the spot to be in, now it was just run down and straight hood. I liked hood. How I was born and raised. But when I went to the mall, I wasn't trying to feel that way and have that kind of vibe.

I needed to get some money up to be able to pay my crew that I was about to lead into battle. Now if it was anybody else, I would just kick in the front door A Team style and start taking niggas out. But this was Zeno. This was different. Very different. But it had to be done. I had to get what was mine back.

Since this was different I decided to go about it a different way and meet with Zeno, face to face. Who knows, maybe he didn't want a war. Maybe if I made him an offer he couldn't refuse, he would back down and there wouldn't have to be any bloodshed as a result.

I called him up and asked him to meet up at the place of his choice so we could talk. Truth be told, Zeno had done a good job of running things since I had went down. He expanded our area, we had double the area of coverage now. I actually needed a guy like him to be on my team, not fighting with him for the control of it all. I planned to relay that to him in this meeting. He chose Ultimate Bar and Grill to meet probably for the pat down security no doubt.

Ebony Chronicles of Elevation

My headstrong nephew drove me to where this Ultimate Bar and Grill place was. Had to because it was not around when I was out and I had no idea of how to start to get there. Xay had jumped the gun on this thing and ruined the whole element of surprise. Now Zeno knew I was coming and what I was coming for. Once I reclaimed my streets, I knew I would have to keep an eye on him. He was hungry, real hungry and I couldn't see him sitting quiet and accepting his role as sergeant or lieutenant for long. Naw, he wanted to be the king and even though I knew he respected me, his greed and envy would at some point give him the same courage the cowardly lion with looking for in the Wizard of Oz.

It didn't take Dionne Warwick to tell me that he and I would bump heads at some point in the future. But I didn't have time to worry about all of that now. Now I needed him to ride with me into battle. I knew he wasn't scared to bleed, kill, or die. If it came to that, I needed as many of them as possible. I didn't want to see bloodshed, but I was prepared for the worst.

After being patted down by the big brother at the entrance, I strolled in with my crew chewing on a straw from a soda I was drinking earlier. I use to run through three packs a day easy. Zeno and his crew were already there and seated. All the way in the back. Back to the wall and nothing behind him. Able to see everything from all angles.

Just like I taught him.

He had six guys sitting with him and probably at least three more throughout the place, probably one at the bar and two more at both exit doors.

Once again, just like I taught him.

He stood up and shook my hand as I walked up to the table, showing the respect that he was taught along the way by somebody, probably his grandma in Florida. I appreciated that. Just because we were about to get it on didn't mean we couldn't be respectful and cordial of one another.

"How's it going Zeno?"

Sitting back down as he answered, he replied "Pretty good, no complaints."

"I appreciate you agreeing to meet with me under these circumstances. First off, let me say that I want to thank you for holding down the block while I did my bid."

Zeno didn't speak, but nodded his head in agreement of what I had just said.

"But now that I am out, things can go back to normal. I am prepared to take things off your hands, but as a show of my gratitude, you can keep Campbellton and whatever you decide to start up is cool, as long as I get my customary ten percent. "

Zeno didn't say nuthin, he just leaned back in his chair. But while he was silent, one of his soldiers decided to speak, saying "Man you got my man Zeno fucked up. He made these streets while you was gone. They weren't booming like that then. You done lost your mind if you think...."

Zeno raised his hand and just like that, he stopped, mid sentence and all. Two things I made of that exchange.. One, if he felt confident enough to talk, he had to be one of Zeno's main men because the foot soldiers knew their place and second, Zeno had to have some sort of power to have that cat shut it down so quickly like he did. That was impressive if I do so say myself.

Zeno leaned up in his seat to speak after calming his boy down, who was still visibly upset. "You have to excuse my overzealous sergeant, but he gets very emotional when he feels like someone is trying to take advantage of one of us or strong arming me like it seems like you are doing right now."

I took the chewed up piece of straw out of my mouth and threw it away and said, "Strong arm you? I don't know about that. Remember I gave the streets to you. And based on the fact that you set me up to get knocked off, I don't think that is a bad trade off."

I said that and was probably wrong to do so in front of everyone at the table. It was a low blow and I guess I was trying to discredit him in front of his army. But he didn't flinch at all when he responded back.

"Told you up in Fulton and I'm telling you now, I ain't no damn snitch. You listening to the word of my cousin Larry who owed you money and them fuckin Italians in there, so he would say anything to save his ass."

I almost lost my poker face when Zeno said that. How the hell he know all of that? Could Larry have been lying? I know that I had my doubts, but didn't even consider them I guess, because I wanted so much to get my shit back and needed a reason to have beef with Zeno.

"Whatever, at this point, it is what it is. Bottom line, you have a week to decide what you want to do. You can accept the terms I have laid on the table, or we can go to war. You have the number.

Call me when you decide what you wanna do."

I slowly stood from the table and turned to leave. I had to do so in a hurry before I ended up going back on what I know I needed to do. This was like my son, like I help give birth to him. Definitely didn't want to go to war with him. But it is tough out here in these streets. Sometimes that's just how it goes down. I didn't write the book or make the rules; it just is what it is.

Zeno-

So there it was.

And here I was.

Maxie was out and wanted to get the streets back. All, except one block. One neighborhood. One strip. One hood. All the way back to the spot, my team was screaming that ain't no way in hell we were going out like some bitches. If he wanted a war, then they would bring it to him and give him all he wanted. It was like they were combat soldiers ready to be deployed. Meanwhile, this was exactly what I didn't want. I remember the war Maxi had before he went in. It spilled over way beyond the streets. They started blowing up houses, taking out family members, it was brutal. All I could see since I left Ultimate was my son's smiling face. What would he do without me? I was all he had. Nobody else was here for him, to see about him or protect him from harm. Nobody to teach him about the birds and the bees. Nobody to teach him how to tie his first

Ebony Chronicles of Elevation

tie. Nobody to be there when he graduated from high school and college. Nobody there to tell him, it would be okay the first time a little girl broke his heart or he lost a fight.

He was all I had. I could just see Maxie's crazy nephew Xay trying to hurt my baby. I couldn't have that. I would kill his ass and go turn myself in. But that would leave my little man all alone again. Nope couldn't do it. I had been up all night going back and forth. I had a group of men under me who looked to me for guidance and also for leadership. And I had my son that did the same. I couldn't please both hands, had to make a choice. But when I lined them up, it really was none. I never wanted to be the king. Never wanted to have this on my back. Never planned to sell dope for eight years. Never planned on making 7 figures over that same time either. But I had done both things. And truth be told, I was tired of it. Although I participated in criminal activity, I didn't consider myself to be a crook. I was a good guy, caught up for eight years in a bad situation. I could never pay it back to the people I had hurt. Somewhere down the line, I would no doubt have to answer for it. But until that time, the decision I had to make, that I thought would be an agonizing one, really wasn't.

Stay in the game or Walk Away.

I took out a sheet of paper and a pen and began to write...

Maxie,

By the time you read this, I will be gone. I am sure if you really wanted to find me, you could. At the end of the day, some things are more important than these streets. Than this game. Than all of this money and fame that comes with it. It is different things for different people. For me, it's my son. I am all he has. I can't let him down. Since I now know you kept the streets and the feds off my back for all this time, I know that it would not be a problem for you to send them for me. You know I ain't scared for me, I can handle mine, but I am very scared for my son. It is my job to protect him and so that is what I am going to do. I am going to walk away, leave the game, leave the ATL altogether. The streets that you love so much and are ready to go to war over, are now once again yours. Immediately. I still can't believe you believed my snitch of a cousin over me, but that's cool too. I figured that gave you reason to go on with it. I ain't mad at you, just thought you knew me better. Make sure the streets know I never was a snitch, never will be. Thanks for showing me love, respect and how to play the game. Thanks for sparing my son, I know you could have really made me hurt through him. I hope the streets and the game is all you remember. You may want to keep your nephew Xay because that nigga real hungry and ready to eat...may not be content with not being the man. You will never hear from me again, my life starts brand new first thing tomorrow morning. Think that's it. Take care of my team, they are some good men and will do you well. Let them know I did what I had to do, all for my son because sometimes some things are just that important.

Zeno

I licked the envelope with the name Maxie labeled on it and put it in the mailbox addressed to his house. By the time the Post Office delivered it, I would be long gone.

Broke in Cycles

Moses Miller

Chapter 1

Darnell's gun hand shook rhythmically in the wind, like Muhammad Ali clutching the Olympic torch. The movements were unrelenting and unremitting. His heart fluttered around uncontrollably in his shallow chest as fear embraced him in its evil clutch. What an uncomfortable grip, what an uncomfortable sight. There was no wiggle room to breathe. Paralysis of the mind granted him little time to think.

His eyes scanned the sparse shelves of the small bodega which sat just around the corner from Main Street, in Hempstead. The store was located within close proximity of the bus depot and the Long Island Rail Road station. They kept their doors opened later than most establishments in the area, trying to get that late night loot, in a neighborhood recently ravaged by the recession.

Buddy had just finished gagging the Hispanic store owner and binding his hands tightly with gray duct tape. He was the oldest in the three man crew. Tall, stocky and fearless, his eyes were the opposite of lucid and noticeably lacking of love.

He glanced downward, snarling under his breath. The old man wiggled on the cold dingied tiles, which only spurned Buddy's anger. The kick he delivered to the man's face required little thought or provocation. All movement ceased at that very moment to Buddy's delight.

"I told you I'm not the one to mess with," Buddy yelled, his voice echoing throughout the small store.

Bam was behind the counter emptying the cash register of all the bills. He was Buddy's younger brother. Only a year and Bam's lighter complexion separated the two, who otherwise could pass for twins. As Bam stuffed the crumpled bills in his pocket, he counted a little more than five hundred dollars in his head. It was less than what he had expected, but more than he previously had.

The whole caper took less than ten minutes, as they had planned. It was a quarter to midnight when the three men ran out the store with knitted ski masks concealing their faces. The streets were bare. The sounds of summer's eve were silenced, with the exception of the scarce hum of a car's engine breaking the serenity.

Wallerbee was behind the wheel smoking a Newport when his three partners in crime hopped into the car. He was also wearing a fitted knitted mask, improvising by inhaling smoke through a third hole he made in the front of it.

Darnell assumed the shotgun position, while Buddy and Bam slid into the backseat. The doors were barely closed, before Wallerbee had the stolen Accord in drive and his foot prepared to slam down on the gas pedal. Darnell removed the tight mask from his face, exhaling like Terri McMillan, finally feeling as if he could breathe freely again.

"What you waiting for man? Let's bounce," Buddy hissed impatiently, slamming his hand on the back of the car seat for further emphasis. His deep baritone voice filled the small car.

When Buddy talked, people listened. He had an authoritative tone and an attitude to match. Wallerbee was poised to drive off when he noticed a movement in his peripheral vision. Darnell noticed the same thing at the same time. His body froze and clammed up in the well of

Ebony Chronicles of Elevation

his seat, and once again he began to feel as if he was gasping for air.

A black man with salt and pepper hair was standing on the sidewalk a few feet from the store. He was tall and looked older than he actually was. He had just walked up, making a hasty decision to get a late night snack. Wrong place, right idea. He had a relationship with the owner, and oftentimes found himself at the store late at night, if for nothing more than a conversation. He had seen the men flee and now he was staring blankly into the face of the only unmasked man in the vehicle.

No one moved, seemingly confused by this abnormality. Then Buddy spoke, once again in that deep demanding tone that required your complete attention.

"Handle your business!"

Darnell knew the command was directed at him, but still he didn't move. It was probably the only time he didn't ask, "How high?" when Buddy told him to jump.

"He seen your face. I ain't going back up north because of you. Take care of that!"

There was no denying Buddy's demands twice. Darnell knew this. Suddenly, the sawed off shotgun sitting in his lap felt like a ton of bricks. But, somehow he moved. He managed to open the door and step outside. Now he was standing ten feet away from the older black man, looking at him eye level.

Darnell's hand invoked Parkinson's again. His throat sandpaper dry. It took every bit of strength he had to level the shotgun. The old man stood his ground, unmoved as an eternity passed by in less than a ten second stretch. Then their eyes met for one final time before Darnell mustered up the courage to squeeze his sweaty finger on the trigger, waiting to hear the sound that manifests death.

Chapter 2

Shalonda Fairbanks was only twenty-two and a half, with a five-year-old son and a five year plan. Her dark complexioned skin was mostly unblemished, sans a couple of wrinkle lines from premature stress. Her body still curved in the same places that helped her become the most popular cheerleader on the Hempstead High School squad, although the birth of her son had also blessed her with a few unsightly stretch marks.

She was always cute in the face, but never drop dead gorgeous. Shalonda had a tight package that was plump in all the right places. From an early age she was blessed with the physical attributes needed to turn more than a few heads.

As she sat on her lumpy twin mattress, the cheerleading days of the past seemed like an eternity ago. Her prior life ended when a sprouting seed was placed in her young fertile belly. Oftentimes, she sat alone in the small basement studio apartment which she called home for the past two years wondering where she had gone wrong.

The moist basement reeked of mildew as she inhaled air that was contaminated with mold. She had recently read about the symptoms brought on by the inhalation of mold spores and was convinced it was the reason sickness continuously plagued her and her son. Demontay was only five, and he had already been diagnosed with asthma and seemed to have a respiratory infection every other month.

A loud hum in an adjacent room was followed by the rattling of the copper pipes which were strewn in a maze like pattern on the basement's low hanging ceiling. This was their only source of heat. The scent of burning oil would follow shortly, along with a constant reminder of how low Shalonda's life had actually sunk.

Ebony Chronicles of Elevation

The basement of the two level cape had its own separate entrance and stairs leading to the rear of the house. The only set of windows allowing visibility outside provided a partial view of the backyard. In her spare time she'd daydream, gazing into the nothingness that greeted her eyes. This time she was staring with a purpose, while she waited for the person to arrive who she had just watched descend the concrete stairs.

Seconds later, the deadbolt disengaged and the basement door swung inwardly. Then in walked Darnell, with a Mcdonald's bag and a small teddy bear in his hand, overshadowed by the sheepish grin on his face. Cold air followed him inside, even as moist sweat dripped down his face. He locked the door behind him, all the while feeling Shalonda's peering eyes following his every move.

"Where's my little man? I told you to keep him up for me," Darnell said, peering around the room, spotting his son sleeping in a small toddler bed against one of the walls.

Shalonda sucked her teeth before saying, "Are you serious, Darnell? Do you know what time it is?"

"I told you to keep him up so I could celebrate his birthday with him. Damn, you couldn't even do that?"

Shalonda stood up from her bed with arched eyebrows and a piercing glare. "His birthday was yesterday, Darnell. It's almost one in the morning. Where the hell you been? Did you think I was going to keep him up all night waiting on your sorry behind?"

"Yo, you need to stop all of that yapping. You always running off at the mouth like you got vocal diarrhea or something. Meanwhile, I'm out here doing what I can to provide for you two. You know how much I be sacrificing for you, Ma? Damn, you're an ungrateful little b—"

"Ungrateful? Sacrifice?" Shalonda interrupted, before she reached out and attempted to snatch the McDonald's bag from Darnell's hand. The white bag ripped open. Then cold French fries, a cheese burger and a happy meal toy still wrapped in plastic fell to the floor by her feet.

"Oh, that's how you sacrifice, huh? You bought your son a happy meal for his birthday and you want a father of the year award," Shalonda let out a snide laugh. "Oh, I'm sorry. I forgot the nice little teddy bear you got him as well. I bet you want a little medal don't you?"

Fury engulfed Darnell. Her words cut through him in a slow methodical slice that tore to the core. He wanted to hit her if only to shut her up. He wanted her to physically feel the pain her words were causing him emotionally. But, he didn't, because he couldn't.

When he was growing up, he had seen so many men put their hands on his mother that he vowed to never be like them. So instead, he tried to think of just the right words to use to make her feel like less of a woman. In his mind, he thought about all the other women he could be with who wouldn't ask for much more than his time. He thought of all the places he'd rather be, if only to escape.

"You're a sorry excuse for a father," Shalonda muttered with a shake of her head. "At this point, I know you don't care about me. Your actions show you don't give a damn about me. I mean, how many times did I call you earlier, and all I got was your voicemail."

"I was busy."

"Busy doing what, Darnell?"

"I was busy. That's all you need to know," he spat back.

Shalonda shrugged her shoulders and replied, "You're right. I don't need to know where you were. I don't even care about you. But, he does. And you know what? He doesn't deserve this, because he didn't ask to be here."

"And what do you want me to do?"

Ebony Chronicles of Elevation

"I want you to be a man. I want you to be a father. All he wanted today—*yesterday* was for his father to be with him on his birthday, and you couldn't even do that."

"But, I'm here now. That's why I asked you to keep him up for me. I was going to surprise him with the happy meal, but I was going to buy him a bike tomorrow," Darnell replied, flashing a wad of bills he had just retrieved from his pocket.

Shalonda shook her head again, "You just don't get it. The money don't mean a thing to him and neither does the teddy bear, the happy meal or the bike. All he wanted was you. Is that too much to ask?"

Darnell threw the only piece of the bag remaining in his hand to the floor in frustration. Then he wiped his brow, while his head began to ache where his eyebrows furrowed.

"Do you know how much I do for you and that little dude? I didn't even know my pops when I was growing up. I didn't get no money from him or none of that. And here I am bustin' my butt so yawl can eat and this is what I get in return. I don't even know why I bother."

"Well, if you don't know, then I'm not going to be the one to tell you."

Darnell shrugged his shoulders and said, "You always got something smart to say out of your mouth, yo. All that I do, man."

"Just because you do a little more than a little bit, it doesn't make it a lot," Shalonda replied nonchalantly as she glared into his face.

Darnell reached for the door handle and undid the deadbolt. Fuming inside, he grabbed the wad of money out of his pocket and threw the crumpled bills in Shalonda's face. The action caught her by surprise. Before she could react, Darnell slammed the basement door and bolted up the concrete steps outside.

He didn't look back, driven by anger bubbling up inside of him. His pride was feeding his emotions, telling him to find another woman to lay up with for the night. That's how he would get Shalonda back. That was how he would regain his manhood after being so handedly emasculated.

Cold wind from the wintry night greeted his face. It felt soothing on his hot and sweaty skin. The house where Shalonda lived was around the block from Greenfield Cemetery, on a side street. He hated cemeteries, because they reminded him of death. His grandmother was buried at Greenfield. That was an excuse he used oftentimes when he didn't come home. When all else failed, he'd put it on his disdain for death and not wanting to be around his deceased grandmother.

A Lincoln Town Car from the late eighties was the only wheels Darnell had to get around. It was a gas guzzler, but pretty reliable nonetheless. The insurance premium had gone unpaid for the past five months. He became accustomed to driving dirty, tactically using the side streets to avoid the police at all costs.

Shalonda's scathing words had been on his mind for his entire trek down the street, to the place where he had parked his car. But, as he neared the old blue sedan his instincts swiftly began to kick in. A man was standing near his car. The shrouded darkness hid him partially, making him look even more out of place.

Darnell crossed the quiet suburban street, already deciding to walk past the car to better assess the situation. Something wasn't right. He barely made it onto the adjacent sidewalk when he heard his name being yelled. It was his full government name, which couldn't be good.

His first thought was to run, but then another voice urged him not to move, as if it was reading his mind. Before he could react, he felt a sharp blow of a night stick against the back of his legs, causing him to collapse. Then he felt the pain of someone's knee piercing his back, before his hands were tightly cuffed and his *Miranda* rights were read.

Chapter 3

For Walter Givens, weekday mornings usually consisted of a light breakfast and a few casual games of bingo at the American Legion hall. He wasn't retirement age yet, but health issues kept him from the nine to five grind for the past year. Spending time with the senior citizens was always a nice change of pace. He didn't hang around just to hustle them, although he could have with relative ease. Truth be told, he truly enjoyed their company.

This morning, he made a conscious decision to forego the bingo circuit. Last night, he had faced a near brush with death. Seeing a shotgun pointing down on him didn't leave him fearful. Contrarily, he wasn't afraid of dying. However, he did observe the look in the young boy's eyes as he struggled to level his weapon.

The look he was greeted with was one of fear and indecisiveness. Walter knew all too well that those two elements mixed together made for one dangerous concoction. Somehow, by the grace of God, the gun hadn't fired. There was also an eerie familiarity about the young man that he observed as well.

The incident had led Walter to make two unlikely trips within the past three hours. Under the bequest of the boys in blue he was down at the 1st Precinct shortly after sunrise. Standing uncomfortably behind a one-way glass, he positively identified the young man who had failed to take his life only hours earlier. And now he was sitting in the family room of Second Shiloh Baptist church, across from Bishop Kincaid.

It was just after eight in the morning, but the Bishop was wide-eyed. He wore a charcoal gray three-piece suit matching his eyes, which was an odd eye color for a man with a complexion as dark as his. Walter hadn't dressed to impress for the occasion. It was hard enough for him to even set foot in the religious institution, let alone meet with the Bishop.

The last time he had been here, he shared a few choice words with the Bishop. As a matter of fact, in front of the entire congregation he boldly told the man of the cloth to, "Kiss my black behind where the sun don't shine." It was at his wife's funeral and it could have been a whole lot worse. Out of respect for the house of the Lord he kept his comments pure and purged of the profanity he really wanted to use.

There were no apologies when Walter showed up this morning and no love lost between the two men. The outburst had come at a time when Walter was questioning if there was truly a God. However, the events that unfolded over the past few hours had left him believing once again in the man upstairs. Something or someone had saved his life. And if something or someone had saved his life, it had to be for some good reason.

The men spoke about many things, segueing from topic to topic naturally. Walter asked about God, the Creator's purpose and how mankind fit into the whole scheme of things. The answers were all things he had heard in the past, and already knew. Then he brought up the sins of his past, which was the real reason he found himself at the church today. The near death experience had given him a revelation, peeling back the Band-Aids on some emotional wounds that had never healed.

"God works in mysterious ways, Walt. You know sometimes it's obvious, but on other occasions it may take some time for the true meaning to be revealed," Bishop

Kincaid said before taking a sip from a coffee mug in front of him.

"I know all of that, but I also believe that everything happens for many reasons. You decide what you take from it, what it means and what it becomes," Walter stated.

The two men shared a history that dated back many years. They knew each other before Kincaid got the call and took on his new role in the community. They didn't always see eye to eye, but with history, there was also a certain amount of respect.

"There's such limited time, you know? I mean, obviously if I could change some things from the past I would. However, you know that's not even an option," Walter said somberly.

"Of course. That's one of mankind's ongoing dilemmas...looking backwards while life is steady moving ahead rapidly. In a car, the rearview mirror is smaller than the windshield, just so we spend more time looking in front of us than behind."

Walter nodded his head and replied, "That's true, but it's easier said than done."

"The challenge is figuring out where you fit in. Use those sins from the past to motivate your sain'tly duties going forward."

Chapter 4

The news of Darnell's arrest didn't take long to germinate through the hood. Before noon, Buddy had gotten the word. He linked up with Bam and Wallerbee before holing up at one of his girlfriend's apartments who lived further away than around the way. He knew Darnell couldn't be flipped, but he also knew what was obvious as well. A crew four deep had robbed the bodega. It wouldn't take much for Five-0 to figure out who had been with Darnell.

A small apartment in the Roslyn projects was where they took root. This block long set of two-story buildings was cut out of the predominately affluent white community. It was far from the typical projects, but its inhabitants embraced the moniker with open arms. The seclusion provided the perfect backdrop for Buddy to formulate a plan without fear of the police finding out where he was. He always thought well on his feet, staying one step ahead of his foes.

Bam paced back in forth in the small apartment. He didn't have his brother's brain, but he wasn't lacking when it came to brawn. He was also full of the fearlessness young men inherently had. Bam had no fear of killing, dying or even the threat of getting shot.

"I can't believe that dude took off his mask. That's just mad dumb, know what I mean?" Bam said. "I mean, I ain't trying to kick that dude when he's down, but that ain't G. That ain't game. In a way, he deserved what he got.

Buddy's shoulders stiffened as he glared at his brother. "Yo, don't say that. Don't let me ever hear you say somebody deserves to be locked in the belly of the beast."

Sensing his brother's irritation, Bam backtracked by saying, "I didn't mean he deserved it, but I just think that we could have done a better job or he should have done a better job, rather."

"Yeah, he slipped," Buddy acknowledged. "But, ain't nobody expect that old man to snitch."

"He wouldn't be alive if Dee would have just blasted him like you told him," Wallerbee added, joining the conversation for the first time.

"Yeah, but his gun jammed," Buddy retorted.

"Or so he said," Bam replied sarcastically.

Ebony Chronicles of Elevation

Buddy's face screwed up and his eyes went from Bam to Wallerbee and then back to his brother again. "What, yawl think he's lying?"

Both boys shrugged, but neither commented.

"Listen, we don't even have time to be thinking like that. What we do know for sure is that Dee is locked down and there's an old man singing to the pigs, like messing with swine is good for you—ya, dig?"

"So, what you want to do about that?" Bam asked.

"What you think?" Buddy replied with a devious grin.

"We need to send him a little message?" Wallerbee asked.

Buddy smirked. "Nah, when people send messages, they usually wait around for a response. I don't want that old man running his mouth no more."

Chapter 5

From a holding cell, Darnell was transported to a courthouse in Mineola, where he stood in front of a judge with a court appointed attorney. The whole process went rather quickly and before he knew it, he was back sitting in a van filled with other inmates, being whisked away to Carmen Avenue, in East Meadow.

East Meadow was where the Nassau County Jail was located. And that was where Darnell was, sitting in another cell. He had been here before, on multiple occasions. The first two times were misdemeanors, and he managed to avoid being sent to the prison facilities upstate.

The latest charge was a b-felony, and with his record there was no way he was going to avoid that up north trip. His only wish was that he ended up in a minimum security prison. Prison had a way of making the sane become savage. And the worst kind of inmate was one who had been a savage long before he had entered the devil's den.

Since Darnell was a juvenile, he had been in and out of institutions. He received evaluations, tests and even had his DNA analyzed. The end result was the belief that he suffered from acute neurosis and manic depression. They said it stemmed from the physical and emotional abuse he had received as a child.

Darnell found the feedback to be rewarding. It let him know exactly how they expected him to act, so he manipulated people based on their preconceived notions. The truth was that in his mind, the only issues he acknowledged were the fragile relationships he had with his mother and the various men that were in and out of his life.

His mother's boyfriend was the one who taught him how to fight and shoot guns when the need arose. Another guy she dated taught him how to inhale weed from a blunt. That was Darnell's tenth birthday, which he remembered like it was yesterday. The same man taught him how to run game on girls. Darnell had been following his words of wisdom ever since.

What he had been told was to, "Never handcuff no hoe." And all girls were hoes. So, that was the philosophy he used with every female he dealt with in the past. Being a player was a hit and run operation. He was taught to be with as many females as he could game, and stick and move like he was running from Five-O. There was no room for catching feelings.

Shortly after arriving inside the pen, Darnell ran into a few acquaintances from Hempstead. They made sure he was straight with some items from commissary, knowing it might be a while before his own people sent him a package. He appreciated the gesture, but wasn't quite ready to make himself at home just yet. However, when a young dude named Baby Vince shared a *Newsday* clipping with him, the reality of the situation started to set in.

Ebony Chronicles of Elevation

In the pen, it didn't take much to get recognition. While the people he knew were giving him props for making it into *Newsday*, all he could think of is that a serious case also meant serious time. And making it to *Newsday* meant that he was facing just that.

Chapter 6

In the mornings before the sun had fully risen, Shalonda used the heat from the oven to keep the basement warm. Besides the warmth from the exposed pipes, she relied on extra blankets to stay warm. However, on certain days, it was just too cold outside. And on those occasions she had to use the oven, even though she had been warned about doing so on several occasions by her landlord.

Demontay awakened with a runny nose and a congested chest. When he spoke it was through a wheeze, the rattling in his chest obvious and upsetting. After cleaning his nose, Shalonda retrieved the nebulizer and gave him a treatment of Albuterol. He inhaled the thick mist from the mask, coughing as his lungs opened up. As the phlegm loosened, his breathing stabilized and his wheezing dissipated.

"What do you want for breakfast, little man?" Shalonda asked, squeezing one of her son's pudgy cheeks.

Demontay was the spitting image of his father. They both had dimples in both cheeks, light complexioned skin and an infectious personalities. Their eye lashes were long enough to make any female envious, with deep brown pupils that warmed your heart with every gaze. It was impossible to see Demontay without seeing Darnell and vice-versa.

"Can I have a peena bunna and jelly sandwich?" Demontay asked.

"Peanut butter and jelly? You always want peanut butter and jelly," Shalonda replied.

Demontay smiled revealing his dimples and ecstatically said, "I love peena bunna butter and jelly sandwiches."

"I know you do, but you can't eat peanut butter every day."

"Please," Demontay said, again flashing his infectious smile. It was the same facial expression his father made when he wanted something. It was the look that forced her to accept Darnell's advances, and ultimately resulted in Demontay's conception.

"Okay, but this is the last time. You had peanut butter everyday this week," Shalonda said, giving in.

She hadn't slept well last night. The argument with Darnell had left her angered and full of adrenaline. All she could think about was the mistakes she had made and how quickly life was passing her by. Before she met Darnell, she had dreams of being an LPN and eventually going on to be a physical therapist. Now, she was trying to find the right program to attend to obtain her GED. The friends she had when she got pregnant had already graduated and gone on with their lives.

"Is daddy comin' home today?" Demontay asked.

He loved his father, even though he was barely around. When he was, the two were tied at the hip. Their bond made Shalonda envious at times. She was the only one who cared for Demontay when he was sick. She read to him at night and made all of his meals, but still he always had a need for his father. What angered her even further was that Darnell didn't appreciate how much his son needed him. He didn't deserve Demontay's love.

"No, daddy won't be here today."

Ebony Chronicles of Elevation

"Why? He said he was gonna get me a big toy for my birthday."

Shalonda glanced across the table at the teddy bear Darnell brought with him earlier. The crumpled Mcdonald's bag was still lying on the floor where he had thrown it.

"Daddy had to go away for work."

It was a lie she had used so often that Demontay had come accustomed to hearing it. He hated work or "business" as his mother had often called it. He didn't know what it meant other than the fact that he wouldn't be seeing his father for awhile.

"He said he was gonna be here for my birthday."

Seeing him sad melted Shalonda's heart. She was always the bearer of the bad news. Darnell never had to go through the agonizing moments that pulled on your heart strings. All he had to do was come around, toss Demontay in the air a few times or buy him a toy and it would be as if all was forgiven.

"Daddy, wanted to be here, but he couldn't. His job called him at the last minute," she lied.

Demontay looked her in the face, his young eyes taking it all in. As young as he was, he seemed to comprehend more than the average child his age. He never accepted the first response, and always seemed to ask for further clarification to glean a more complete understanding.

Finally he asked, "When is he comin' back?"

"I don't know. He said he would call," Shalonda responded, before cutting the peanut butter and jelly sandwich she had just prepared into two triangles and placing the small plate that held them in front of her son.

Demontay didn't inquire further, and she was glad. Darnell had called her earlier in the morning from the precinct, asking her to do the same thing she had done on several other occasions. He told her to call everyone they knew and get up some bail money. She followed the routine, calling upon friends and family who for the most part were struggling just like they were.

As a last resort she called, Buddy, who was somehow already aware of what happened. Shalonda never liked him and limited their conversations, wishing that Darnell would do the same. She knew that as long as they were friends, Darnell would never walk away from the streets that eventually had a way of destroying anyone who swore allegiance to them.

Buddy told her not to worry about it, or rather he said, "Don't even sweat that, Ma. I got this." She didn't ask him to elaborate further, not sure she even wanted to know the details. However, something didn't sit well with her after that conversation, and she still had a nagging feeling that things were going to get bad before they got any better.

Chapter 7

A cold freeze settled upon the entire state of New York earlier in the day, which was a prelude to the fierce frigidness of the evening that followed. They described it as a nor'easter that had blown in from Canada. For late January, this wasn't unusual. However, the winter had been fairly mild up to this point leaving most people ill prepared.

Walter lived in a small house just off of North Franklin Avenue near the borderline separating Hempstead from Garden City. The differences between the two communities could not have been more obvious or purposely devised. One community was dirty and one was pristine, flourishing and clean. One had what many believed was one of the worst school districts in the county,

Ebony Chronicles of Elevation

and the other was arguably one of the better educational systems in the state. There was no surprise that one neighborhood was predominately inhabited by blacks and Latinos while the other was almost exclusively white.

Two old kerosene heaters kept Walter's small home comfortable. The bigger of the two heaters sat downstairs in the living room just at the base of the steps, so the warm air could rise. A cast iron pot half-filled with tap water sat on top of it, in order to reduce the soot emission and add some moisture to the air as well.

The orange flame from the heater flickered and cast a formidable shadow on the wall in Walter's bedroom, while he sat in his bed looking through old copies of Popular Mechanics magazines. He was a car buff, although he hadn't driven in years. His last car was a turbo charged Mustang, which he'd race down the Meadowbrook Parkway in his leisure. Cataracts killed his racing career, but not before the Feds had confiscated his car collection.

As a young man, Walter had jumped around from hustle to hustle, until he finally found something complimentary to his talents. He liked people, was very articulate and had the gift of gab. So naturally, he became a used car salesman. However, Hempstead was home to over a dozen dealerships. Faced with fierce competition, he came up with an idea to sell high end sports cars with a twist. His lot had Ferraris, Lambos, Mazzaratis and Porches. The twist was that they were all stolen. The VIN tags were flawlessly removed and replaced in an elaborate operation as far reaching as California.

Providing exquisite vehicles to the bourgeois businessmen in Garden City brought in good money fast. This would have been more than enough to retire on, if someone hadn't gotten pinched and started singing like Rihanna. Walter ended up serving six-years, which was a blessing based on what the judge had originally wanted to give him. The same network he had been affiliated with was also moving major drugs through the same channels. Fortunately, Walter's lawyer had effectively fought to have him tried separately from the other defendants who were primarily involved in the drug operation.

A knock at the front door of the house seized Walter's attention. It was after nine in the evening, which was too late for visitors. He didn't mind solicitors. They broke up the monotony, and he was always game for a good debate. However, there were just certain things that you didn't do, which included coming to a man's house after dark unannounced.

The kerosene was most effective in enclosed areas, which meant the bedroom was toasty. The hallway was bordering on chilly, but things warmed up again once he reached the bottom of the steps. The flickering light from the heater guided Walter to the front door. He undid the deadbolt, pausing as he thought to ask who was actually outside.

"Who is it?" Walter asked, receiving no response.

"Who is it?" He inquired a second time, hearing a faint noise on the other side of the door. Growing impatient, he hastily undid the chain lock poised to give whoever was playing games a piece of his mind. The door was partially cracked when it came crashing all the way in.

Caught off guard, Walter didn't have time to plant his feet as the shoddy wooden door collided against his forehead, knocking him dizzily to the floor. His eyes struggled to focus as he tried to comprehend what had just taken place. He glanced upwards at the wall, focusing in on a picture of him and his deceased son, Marvin. It was taken a week before he was killed.

Walter was still staring at the picture on the wall when the first masked man entered his house. The flickering from the kerosene heater cast an ominous

Ebony Chronicles of Elevation

shadow on the wall as the stocky man hovered over him. In his hands he held a shotgun, but he was in no rush to level it. Through the holes in the mask he followed Walter's eyes to the picture on the wall. Then in a slow methodical movement he pointed his shotgun toward the old man lying on the floor quietly in submission.

"Snitches end up in ditches, old man," were the only words Buddy uttered as he focused in on his fallen prey.

Chapter 8

The District Attorney's office belabored the convenience store robbery case for five months, searching for anything that could validly be introduced as evidence to justify going to trial. Without an eyewitness' account and identification of the primary suspect, it would be nearly impossible to convince a jury to convict. So with deep reluctance, the case was thrown out and Darnell became a free man again just as the summer began.

Over the past five months, it had been Shalonda who consistently visited him each week in the County jail and took up most of his phone time. Most of his boys couldn't come up to the jail, without violating their probation, and they didn't write either. He had plenty of letters to read, but they all came from his baby's mother.

The letters from Shalonda were very intimate and heart wrenching. She bared her soul, in so many words revealing all of her fears and concerns. She wanted them to be a family and she needed him to change. To his credit, Darnell said all the right things, like only he knew how. He promised to be a new man when he got home. He professed that he had finally realized what he had and didn't want to jeopardize losing it ever again.

It was on a Friday afternoon when he would finally taste freedom again. The air was always more refreshing on the other side. With the first breath you inhale after escaping captivity, your psyche and priorities immediately change. The first thing on Darnell's agenda was a welcome home party his boys had planned for him. It was to be held at club Taboo in West Hempstead. Buddy had rented out the V.I.P. section to celebrate his return.

Bam and Wallerbee took him to Green Acres mall so he could get right. They had new money from a credit card scheme someone put them on to, and they were more than willing to share with their homie who was fresh out the pen and in dire need of some new gear. They spent a couple of hours at the mall hitting up Foot Locker and Excel for the latest clothing styles. Afterwards, they hollered at some females before catching up over some wings and fries at Applebees.

Between shopping, eating and just talking, the day passed by rather quickly. Before long it was dark outside as evening settled in. They ended up at Wallerbee's crib which was in an area of Hempstead called the Heights. They all shared a swisher with his mother before settling down in the living room to play Black Ops on his X-Box. Bam headed out, promising to catch up with them later that night.

Darnell had an inkling to call Shalonda, but decided against it. She'd just pester him with questions and concerns which he didn't want to hear. Right now, he just wanted to enjoy life and live in the moment. When he saw her tomorrow, he'd lie and tell her his paperwork got lost or something.

Besides, Wallerbee had invited some girls from Glen Cove over. They were young, thirsty and impressionable. It didn't take much convincing for them to have their way with them after they all got high together. They ran some game and dropped them off in Glen Cove before heading over to Club Taboo. People traveled from as far as the city

Ebony Chronicles of Elevation

to go to this club that was notorious for booking B-list celebrities.

Buddy was standing behind a round table in the VIP section of the club, talking to a small crowd that was gathered around him when they arrived. He was too animated and full of energy to sit still. Three bottles of *Ace of Spades* champagne were on chill in front of him, which he ignored momentarily. He was too focused on his story and his crowd. He didn't even notice Darnell as he approached and settled in. Wallerbee stayed behind in the body of the club, eyeing a group of females posted up by the bar.

"My dude. I shoot first and ask question last, cause yawl know that's why most of these so called gangsters pass," Buddy said with emphasis, plagiarizing a lyric from the Notorious B.I.G. "I let five off in duke, catching him above or below his vitals like a marksman, my dude. I didn't wanna kill him, I just wanted to cripple him. Now he be walking funny style like he playing hopscotch by himself."

Buddy let out a burst of laughter which was followed by a chorus of applause. People laughed who didn't even find the joke funny, solely for his approval. Buddy had that effect on people. They wanted to please him at any cost.

"Hopscotch, my dude. Hopscotch," Buddy added for further emphasis. His smile lit up, then quickly faded as he noticed a face in the crowd which changed his whole demeanor.

"Yo, I can't believe my eyes. My other brother is home." Buddy dramatically stated before pushing through the crowd to get closer to Darnell. "Look at you, Dee. You look like you did that time doing a handstand or something. It was nothing, right?"

"It was hella easy," Darnell replied, feeling the eyes of those watching him.

"Yo, pop that bubbly for my dude. We gotta have a drink for one of the realest soldiers I know," Buddy demanded.

There was always an air around Buddy that drew people to him, that was rarely matched by anyone else in the room.

"Yo, you looking mad good, healthy and all that," Buddy said, before pausing to look Darnell up and down. "No homo, my dude. I know you just got home, so you might take those words to heart and try to wife me or something."

Darnell playfully punched him in the shoulder and said, "You stupid."

Buddy replied by delivering a counterpunch to Darnell's chest which came unexpectedly. "Protect yourself at all times, or you'll end up like that kid Mayweather knocked out," Buddy said sarcastically before pouring bubbly into the wine flutes on the table.

Most of Buddy's soldiers were in the house, posted up in the VIP like they were stars in the hood. Montana, John Carlo, Mossberg, Fendi, Munchie and Stink grabbed a glass, raising their hands as he made a toast in honor of Darnell. Sham was the smallest and youngest in the crew. He held a wine glass in his small hand and played the back, observing more than anything else. Bam was noticeably missing.

The tension in the velvet rope separating the VIP room had been relaxed a little to allow some females with eager eyes to meander amongst the made men. They gravitated toward Darnell, wondering why he was the man of the moment. The attention made him feel good and the alcohol soothed his nerves. Darnell had felt slightly on edge since arriving at the club and couldn't shake the feeling. Ominous thoughts were usually followed by similar

Ebony Chronicles of Elevation

circumstances. He wondered if there was any validity to how he was feeling.

"Yo, you know I don't step inside no pens and I don't do the phone calls either. But, you got my kite, right?" Buddy whispered into Darnell's ear as he stood with his arm around him.

"Yeah, Lakim from the Heights told me that you said you was gonna take care of everything for me. I didn't know what he meant and I still don't. I'm just glad to be home."

Buddy smirked. "I had to take care of that old man who seen the jux go down."

Darnell's face dropped. "You killed him?"

"I snuck up on that dude like a sniper in Black Ops."

"Damn."

"I kicked his old ass to the ground and made him beg for his life. He was crying, nose running, pissy drawers and the whole nine. It was funny as hell."

"Then you killed him?"

"Yo, I raised my baby up and pointed it at his head like that dude did at the end of Scarface," Buddy said, acting out the scene in animated fashion. "But, then I saw a picture on his wall."

"A picture?"

"Yeah, remember, Mega? Older head who used to hustle out of the MLK projects and push all them bad whips and bad honeys?"

"Yeah, he was crazy cool. Like our parent's age. He would always buy us candy and ice cream when he saw us playing out on the block when we was just youngn's."

"Exactly," Buddy replied with a nod. "Homie was hella cool until them El Salvodoreans put his insides on his outsides a few years back."

"So, what does that have to do with the old man?"

"That was his son. That's crazy, right? I told him I was gonna give his old ass a pass on the strength of Mega, but he had to take back his police statement."

"What he say?" Darnell asked curiously.

"Yo, old head got crazy balls. He said he'd tell the police he lied, but he wanted to talk to you face to face when you got home."

"For what?"

"I don't know. I didn't even ask, because I really didn't care. As long as he did what I told him, that's all that mattered," Buddy said, pausing before sarcastically adding. "I heard Mega's old man was pretty tough himself back in the days. He *mighta* wanted to shoot a fair one with you or something. You ever feel how hard old people's knuckles is?"

A disturbance in the club diverted Buddy's attention. He glanced away from Darnell and peered into the rambunctious crowd. Most people were dashing for the exit, but amidst the mayhem there were a dozen or so figures moving momentously forward like men motivated to engage in modern warfare.

"Parkside," Buddy spewed beneath his breath, before glancing in Darnell's direction as a glass flew past his head barely missing him.

Just home from jail, the serenity that should be synonymous with a club suddenly resembled the belly of the beast he had so willingly departed. There were guerrillas in the midst, heading briskly towards the VIP section with ill conceived intentions.

Wallerbee was nowhere to be found, undoubtedly out in the range where the evil was evident. Darnell blinked in a literal sense, caught off guard by the chaos. Buddy stood straight backed with a poker face, waiting until the last minute to show his hand. Finally, he revealed a chrome

Ebony Chronicles of Elevation

cannon, which was concealed seconds earlier and a deranged smile.

A reggae song was playing loudly—Something new from Sean Paul. Darnell barely heard it. His eyes were fixated on a shadow in the darkness. The young man leveled his gun, the barrel revealing itself as his finger settled on the trigger. In his mind he moved, scrambling out of the way, but in actuality his body remained frozen like Teddy Pendergrass in his wheelchair.

The blast from Buddy's gun blended in with the heavy bottom from the reggae bass. He focused in on his target, with anticipation which couldn't be simmered by patience. The Desert Eagle spit out a spark before it coughed out a bullet that ripped through a guerrilla's cheek before finding a resting place in a young girl's unsuspecting shoulder.

The high pitched screams that followed were soothing to a shooter. Buddy let off four more rounds which all missed their intended targets. By now, the partygoers were either cowering down on the ground or fleeing into the parking lot. The would-be assailants were right behind them, dodging bullets as they fled the danger.

"Let's bounce," Buddy urged in a relaxed calm. It took a moment for Darnell to snap out of his daze, before he followed Buddy, quickly leaving the VIP section behind.

The interior of the club was still chaotic as stragglers struggling through confusion tried to determine which way to go to avoid the danger. Buddy abruptly stopped in his tracks on the dance floor and glanced downward. His sudden pause surprised Darnell, before his eyes settled in on the cause of his paralysis.

"Is that Wallerbee?" Darnell asked rhetorically, well aware of the answer.

Blood leaked into a well formed puddle from various knife wounds to his lower back and stomach. He wasn't moving and was barely breathing. Instinctively, Darnell bent down to help his fallen friend, but Buddy grabbed him firmly by the shoulder and lifted him back to his feet.

"Leave him. We gotta go."

With reluctance, Darnell followed his command, running behind Buddy and a few of his cronies as they fled from Club Taboo just before the police arrived.

A little after two o'clock in the morning, Shalonda was awakened to the sound of fumbling keys at the entryway to her apartment before the door abruptly opened. She glanced through tired eyes, immediately becoming fearful as she saw the figure move in the shadows. Reaching beneath her bed, she grabbed the wooden handle of a butcher knife and tried to formulate a plan of attack. Before she could spring into action, the door closed and a familiar voice reached her ears.

"Yo, it's me. Have the police been over here?"

"Darnell?" Shalonda asked dumbfounded, as she stood up from her bed, leaving her sleeping son behind. "When did you get out?"

Darnell had expected this question and had already come up with the response. "At the end of the day. The judge kept me up until five minutes before the court closed. Did anybody come over here for me?"

She could hear the urgency in his voice and smell the liquor on his breath.

"What did you do Darnell?" Shalonda asked timidly, certain that she didn't want to know the answer. It didn't take long after she flicked on the light switch to regret her action.

"Whose blood is that on your shirt? Are you hurt? Did you kill somebody?" Once again, Shalonda asked questions she really didn't want to know the answers to.

Darnell glanced down and spotted the blood on the sleeve of his shirt. He cursed under his breath and immediately unbuttoned the garment. Then he began thinking about the void in Wallerbee's eyes when he saw him lying on the floor. After removing the garment from his body, he looked toward Shalonda.

"I didn't kill nobody. This is Wallerbee's blood."

"Is he okay?"

"I don't know. I mean, I don't think so. Somebody stabbed him. I think he's dead."

His words were cold and lacking feeling. His facial expression was noticeably hard. Silence was followed by a tear that rolled down Shalonda's cheek. Her stomach twisted into a knot as her heart spoke in palpitations.

"What happened? Who did that to him?"

"Look, I can't get into all that right now. The police may come over here asking questions. I need you to try and get the blood out of my shirt."

Shalonda grabbed the shirt and headed toward the bathroom, spotting a few more speckles of blood on the sleeve as she walked. Darnell stared into a blank space, his mind residing in his head, but his thoughts in places outside of the room. He clenched his hands into fists and bit down on his upper lip. He knew what had to be done was inevitable. Wallerbee wouldn't die in vain.

When his thoughts returned to his immediate surroundings, he noticed a set of eyes staring at him, with a look of worry written across the face where they resided. Shalonda was still in the bathroom, but his son, Demontay was observing him closely, as he had been doing since shortly after his arrival.

Chapter 9

Darnell arose from bed just as the stars begin to disappear, and was out on the streets in time to greet the sun. He hadn't slept well, which was to be expected, constantly in a tug of war with borrowed time. Thoughts of his own impending death selfishly consumed his thoughts. He had tossed and turned envisioning every conceivable means of his life being taking. In his inner being, he had accepted the fact that the question was no longer if, but rather when the grim reaper would catch up to him.

One of his fears had been confirmed when he met up with Buddy and Bam at their apartment. Wallerbee was dead. It was still early morning, but they decided to pour out a little Hennessey onto the carpeted floor on his behalf. The liquor drowned away the sorrows in the solemn room. It helped them to cope with the loss, providing needed numbness while instigating aggression.

Bam wasn't revealing it, but he was feeling tortured inside. He blamed himself for not making it to the club. In his heart of hearts he felt like his presence would have made a difference. He promised to avenge Wallerbee's death, one way or another.

Alcohol was truth serum. And although they knew how to hold their liquor, they weren't as adept at holding their tongues. It didn't take long for Darnell to find out what the beef was over. Fendi, Munchie, Bam and Wallerbee had robbed a crew from Parkside outside of a house party last weekend. One of them tried to reach for something and Wallerbee shot him. They knew Parkside suspected they were behind it, but there was no way of them knowing Wallerbee had pulled the trigger. They were all wearing masks.

Buddy took a pull from a blunt he just rolled and wheezed out a thought. "Yo, I was watching American Gangster the other night. You ever saw the one with Chaz Williams?"

"Old head, right? Managed Foxy Brown or something?" Darnell replied.

Ebony Chronicles of Elevation

"Yeah. Straight gangster. He used to rob banks like it was nothing," Bam chimed in.

Buddy nodded before replying, "No doubt."

He pulled from the blunt slowly, before passing it to his younger brother. While Bam inhaled, Buddy remained in deep thought. Darnell had seen this expression before and knew something deep was going to follow.

"Yo, I wanna rob that Chase bank in Uniondale. I've been scoping it out for the past two months and I got the routine down to a science. We hit them on the right day and we walk away with forty, fifty grand easy."

Buddy's comment provoked a mere nod from Bam. He was well aware of his brother's revelations and had been with him on many of his trips to the bank over the past few months.

"I was waiting for you to come home, my dude. It was supposed to be me, you, Bam and Wallerbee. But, now with him gone, I may put that dude Fendi on."

Bam sucked his teeth and said, "But you told me he didn't do nothing last night."

"Yeah, but he wasn't holding. I still think he's a good cat and a stand up, dude. When you do something on this level, you don't get caught doing the damn thing. You get caught from people running their mouths. I know I can trust you two and Fendi is built the same way also."

Bam didn't respond, though inside he questioned his brother's call on Fendi. However, he knew better than to challenge him, knowing that once he had his mind set on something, he never changed. Darnell was quiet as well, for other reasons altogether. He had barely savored the taste of freedom and was being asked to put that all in jeopardy. The last thing on his mind was robbing a bank, while he was still mourning the death of his friend.

"You in or not?" Buddy asked, reading the apprehension on Darnell's face. "You look like you're scared."

"I'm good," Darnell replied, the pressure forcing a change in his demeanor. "I was just thinking about Wallerbee, that all."

Buddy grabbed the bottle of Hennessey and poured some more out on his living room floor. "Yeah, we gonna get some payback for our dude, and then we gonna get this money like he would want us to."

Chapter 10

Three shootings occurred over the next five days, resulting in one death of a teenage gang member. The killing garnered two paragraphs in the *Newsday* and the outcry of a community sickened by the rash of violence continuously taking the lives of their youth.

The suburban streets in Hempstead and Roosevelt were hot with summertime heat, a powder keg waiting to blow. An emotional funeral was held for Wallerbee, which ended in an all out brawl on the streets. Chaos hung in the air like a dark cloud.

All the while, Buddy continued planning the bank robbery unfazed. He multi-tasked, playing a street corner general by day and an architect of anarchy at night. Every day he met with Darnell, Bam and Fendi, updating them on the latest developments in his well thought out plan. Everything was set to go down in a week.

An ominous feeling continued to haunt Darnell, wearing him down as the days passed by slowly. He hadn't seen Shalonda or Demontay lately, and really had no desire to. There was too much on his mind and too much going on in the streets. Unlike Buddy, he wasn't built for beef and all

Ebony Chronicles of Elevation

the drama that came along with it. But, that was the company he kept, and he was guilty by association.

Consciously, he stayed away from Parkside, which neighbored the part of town where Shalonda lived. For the most part, he stayed at Buddy's house, getting high and playing videogames. But, even that was getting old. Being cooped up inside the small apartment was making him stir crazy, which was the reason why he found himself taking more chances and roaming the streets while the sun was still hovering above.

Earlier in the day, he visited a couple of his friends in the projects on Terrace Avenue. And now he was walking down South Franklin Avenue, on edge as he constantly looked around him. The street was a busy thoroughfare connecting Hempstead with Garden City. There were mainly car dealerships on this end, with a splattering of Hispanic restaurants. Besides the boys from Parkside, he had to be just as weary of the Spanish boys as well. Beef could come from any direction.

A quick reach in his jacket pocket confirmed that a .22 Buddy had given him was still there. That was the third time he checked on it in the past twenty minutes. The bus terminal was only a couple of blocks away, within walking distance. He was planning on heading to Glen Cove to see one of the girls he met when he got released from the county jail.

"Excuse me," someone yelled from behind him.

It was a male's voice, hoarse and aggressive. Darnell's body tensed and he immediately thought about his gun and if he had to use it. The courthouses were just up the block and police cruisers patrolled this area on a regular basis in the daytime. It wasn't the most opportune place to clash with his enemies, but beef never came when it was convenient.

When Darnell spun around, his eyes were met by a set much older than his own. The old man peered at him with the same intensity he had when he trained his rifle on him that fateful night several months ago. Both men looked at each other longer than they needed to without speaking. Finally, the old man broke the uncomfortable silence.

"Do you know who I am?"

Darnell nodded and nonchalantly replied, "Yeah, I know who you are."

"Do you have anything to say to me?" Walter Givens asked.

Darnell glanced past him nervously eyeing the streets, then looked back at the old man and said, "What did you want me to say, thank you?"

Walter stared at Darnell without responding, delivering a powerful gaze that shot through him. The old man's demeanor exuded confidence that came with age combined with wisdom.

"Have you ever been to the African American Museum?" Walter asked.

The question caught Darnell off guard, since it was so leftfield. Darnell shrugged his shoulders and replied, "Nah, where's that?"

"Its right here," Walter replied, pointing to a building to his right.

Darnell glanced at the structure on the corner, noticing the large block letters on the building's stucco facade identifying it as a museum. He had been past the building a hundred times and never paid attention to what it was before.

"I didn't even know that was there," Darnell said, feeling slightly embarrassed.

Walter chuckled lightly and replied, "Most people don't. They walk past it every day and don't even give it a second thought."

Ebony Chronicles of Elevation

Darnell nodded his head quietly.

Walter grabbed the door handle to the museum and said, "Let's go inside. I know the owner."

He opened the door and stepped inside without waiting for a response from Darnell or looking to see if the young man was going to follow behind him. He was just inside the lobby when a young lady sitting behind the desk greeted him. Her attention immediately shifted to Darnell, as she prepared to ask him for his two-dollar admission fee. However, Walter intervened before she got the words out.

"He's with me."

"Oh, okay, Walter," the brown-skinned twenty–year-old replied with a smile.

They strolled through the modernized museum, glancing over a New Orleans's exhibit. Walter led the way, walking slowly. He stopped near a small rectangular table in the Mosaic Café. Besides a man sitting behind a counter where tea and other refreshments were sold, there was no one else there. Walter sat down at the table first, followed by Darnell, whose back was against the wall providing visibility outside through a set of glass windows.

"It's beautiful in here, isn't it?" Walter asked, looking across the table at his young companion. The multi-colored pastel walls created an aesthetic that was soft and pleasing to the eye.

"Yeah, it's nice," Darnell replied. He was still trying to figure out the old man's angle, but felt slightly at ease. The interior of the museum was a lot safer than the streets. And from his vantage point, he could see everything going on all around him.

"I killed a man before," Walter stated in a firm tone.

His statement caught Darnell's attention. The old man was staring at him again with those hardened eyes. He didn't blink or flinch, and Darnell found himself looking downward just to avoid his glare.

"Have you ever killed anybody before," Walter continued.

"Nah," Darnell replied shaking his head. "Why do you ask?"

"Just curious. You don't seem like a killer, which is probably why you didn't shoot me outside of that store."

"I didn't shoot you because my gun jammed," Darnell replied, still not making eye contact.

Walter snickered and replied, "Your gun didn't jam, which leads me to believe that you either don't know how to use one or you were scared."

"I wasn't scared," Darnell replied defensively, looking into Walter's face.

"If you weren't you should have been. I ain't never met nobody who was about to take somebody's life and they wasn't scared."

Darnell shrugged his shoulders and said, "I don't get scared."

Walter glanced into his face but ignored his comment. Instead he asked, "Why did you rob that store?"

Darnell shrugged his shoulders, but didn't respond.

"You needed money?" Walter asked.

"Yeah, I guess. It's a recession, know what I'm saying? People is starving out here," Darnell replied nonchalantly.

"That's true," Walter stated. "Have you ever robbed anybody else?"

"Nah," Darnell lied, before taking the focus off of himself. "Have you?"

"No, I wasn't into robbing people. I definitely wouldn't steal from a man just trying to make an honest day's pay," Walter said.

"So, you just kill people," Darnell retorted sarcastically.

Walter laughed and replied, "I guess you're right."

Ebony Chronicles of Elevation

"So, why do you think what you did is any better than robbing somebody?" Darnell asked.

"I never said that. There's nothing worse than taking a man's life. You don't come back from that. When you kill somebody, you destroy everything that they could have been."

"So, you regret what you did?"

"I wouldn't be human if I didn't. You don't just walk away from that," Walter said, pausing to gather his words. "Let me rephrase that. You know how people do drive-bys?"

Darnell nodded his head.

"That's a cowardly way of killing. Not as if there's any honor in taking another man's life, but when you're just shooting out of a window, you rarely know if you actually hit your target. And even if you do know, you don't have to stay around and see the effects of what you did up close. Experiencing death is something different altogether. When you take someone's life, a piece of you dies at the same time."

"So, who did you kill?" Darnell asked, inquisitively.

"Somebody who owed me money. I went to jail for manslaughter, because it was accidental. We got to arguing and then we got to fighting. Next thing I know, I'm looking down at him laying in a pool of blood."

Darnell, immediately envisioned Wallerbee, thinking about his friend dying in the club.

"You blame yourself for *that*? Isn't that like self defense?" Darnell asked.

"There's no defense for taking someone's life. It was over money. I could have walked away. What did killing him do anyway? Dead men don't pay debts. So, what did I really accomplish? You know, you and your friends robbed a man with five children who is struggling to just make it by, and almost killed me in the process. Now, I don't know you, but I'm pretty sure that you and your friends don't have any of that money left, and you're probably trying to figure out how you're going to get your hands on some more cash."

Darnell didn't reply, but his thoughts went from thinking about Wallerbee to thinking about Buddy and his plan to rob the bank. His intestines felt like they were shifting inside of him as he sat across from Walter.

"My son had big dreams. He wanted everything and had to have it right now. That instant gratification that most kids want without earning nothing," Walter said, pausing mid-thought. "That's what killed him. That love for material things."

"Your son's name was Mega, right?" Darnell asked.

"Marvin was his name, but they called him Mega," Walter replied weakly.

"How'd he die?" Darnell asked. "I know Mega was a thorough dude."

Walter seemed to ponder over his question momentarily, before he glanced down at his watch. Next, he checked the time against what showed on a clock hanging from the wall, before standing up slowly.

"What happened to my son and the reason why it happened is a long story. It's one I want you to know, and one I think you need to know, but I can't share it now. If you meet me here the same time tomorrow, we can talk further," Walter advised.

The two men shook hands, before Walter abruptly stood up and walked off, leaving his young companion alone in the café. Darnell roamed around perusing the artwork to pass time. When the sun began to set, he left the museum en route to the bus terminal, keeping a keen eye on the streets as he headed to Buddy's apartment.

Chapter 11

A scene from director F. Gary Gray's breakthrough movie *Set it Off* was playing on the flat screen television in Buddy's small living room. The television was just day's old. He got it from Best Buy with a stolen credit card. The DVD was made over a decade ago, but was still one of his favorites. This was the third time he had watched the movie, today alone.

"Check out the way they blast, Luther," Buddy said, referring to a scene when the female characters from the movie kill a man who stole money they had stashed from a bank heist.

"No mercy on nobody that's disloyal," Buddy yelled.

Bam, Darnell and Fendi were also inside the tight haze filled room. They were all high and lethargic, from alcohol and weed smoke. Buddy was the only one focused and the only one standing. He strolled around the room defiantly, quoting scenes he had memorized from the movie. He'd been alternating between Set it Off, Heat and Takers, studying each film as he formulated his own plan for the bank heist.

"We only take big bills, ya dig?" Buddy asked rhetorically. "Forget what you seen in the movies. They put dye packs in bags with the small bills. They don't wanna ruin them hundreds. That's all we take and leave everything else behind."

Most of Buddy's time over the past few days had been consumed by ravenous thoughts. Every day he was recklessly taking his aggression out on the streets. But even while he warred with his enemies, he stayed focused on his divine plan. Nothing was going to stop him from completing this heist. He was convinced that this would be his way up and out of his current situation.

Fendi was young, but he had a good head on his shoulders. Out of everyone in the room, he was the one least likely to be caught in the drama that comes along with the streets. He came from a decent blue collar family and lived with both of his parents. They worked a lot, but still managed to play an active role in his life. However, that love wasn't enough to steer him completely away from the allure of the streets.

Marijuana filled Fendi's lungs, but his mind remained fairly focused through the fog. Unlike Bam and Darnell, he was listening. Buddy had repeated the same things over and over enough for them to sink in just based on repetition alone. He liked the gangster movies just as much as the next person, but he knew how to separate reality from fiction. His father had always told him that when things seemed too good to be true, they usually were. Buddy was painting a picture through rose colored lenses, even though the chances that things would go off without a hitch seemed slim to none.

To avoid his legs falling asleep, Fendi sat up on the lumpy mattress where he had been lounging for the past hour. His wiry frame looked tired and weighed down. Formulating his words carefully in his head, he looked towards Buddy and asked, "How much money do you think we're gonna walk away with?"

Buddy glanced away from the television and replied, "Fifty or sixty g's easy, for less than ten minutes worth of work. We stick to my plan and nobody gets hurt, unless they get in the way. In any case, we all walk away paid."

Being high didn't stop the wheels from spinning around in Fendi's head. Fifty or sixty thousand split between the four of them meant fifteen thousand a piece at the most. The risk hardly seemed worth the reward. But, he knew better than to question Buddy, so he kept his thoughts to himself. However, he did feel compelled to ask,

Ebony Chronicles of Elevation

"How do you know how much money they're gonna have there?"

A sinister smile slowly came across Buddy's face before he replied, "I was wondering when somebody was gonna ask that. You know how the police *thought* Frankie helped with the first robbery in the movie? Well, I really have somebody working for us on the inside."

On the flat screen, Jada Pinkett-Smith and Vivica Fox's characters were discussing the plans for their final bank robbery which would prove to be a fatal one. Buddy had stated "We stick to my plan and nobody gets hurt, unless they get in the way," which was hardly reassuring. Fendi had seen the movie enough times to know how it ended. He just hoped that they avoided the same outcome.

Chapter 12

Walter Givens was at his doctor's office in Rockville Centre first thing in the morning. It was for an appointment with a specialist, which he had reluctantly been to see several times over the past few months. The young Jewish physician was friendly enough, but his prognosis was always the same. Walter was convinced that the appointments were nothing more than a means to bill his insurance company, but he made them all despite his misgivings.

Before noon he was back in Hempstead, playing bingo with his senior citizen friends. He won enough money to cover his lunch and roundtrip bus fare to the doctor. That was indeed a blessing for him. Win or lose, he looked forward to his bingo time.

After doing some reading at the library, he headed over to the African American Museum. As usual, he was greeted at the doorway before being ushered in with no cover charge. It was quiet inside, the midday crowd light as usual. Walter liked it like this. Crowds made him feel claustrophobic and rushed. It was the perfect time for him to peruse the New Orleans exhibit that recently arrived.

The artwork was post Katrina, which provided a refreshing look at the resiliency of a people who had been displaced, misguided and mistreated after one of America's most horrific storms. The vivid oil paintings were a testament to a people, their spirit and pride. Just like the display so boldly expressed, no matter what we've faced as a people, "We Will Rise."

Time passed by quickly as it always did when Walter was inside the museum. He took in the exhibits closely, paying attention to the intricate details. Before he knew it, it was past three o'clock and he had downed three lattés, which were two past his limit. The caffeine had him wired and jittery as he sat at a table in the cafe and consumed his mind with an article he was reading about Adam Clayton Powell, Jr. inside an old Ebony magazine.

In his youth, suspicion would have been aroused instinctively inclining him to steal an upward glance, when the young man first arrived and started observing him from a relatively close distance minutes earlier. Instead, it took a break between paragraphs for Walter's eyes to venture away from the magazine and notice Darnell hovering at the far end of the table.

"Hey. How long you been there?" Walter asked inquisitively, frown lines decorating his forehead.

"Not too long," Darnell replied.

"I didn't think you were gonna come," Walter stated as he closed the old Ebony magazine.

"I told you I'd be here," Darnell replied. The truth was, Darnell didn't plan to come back. Curiosity alone wasn't enough of a motivator to compel him to make this journey. He didn't know what it exactly was. It wasn't as if he cared that much about Mega. He was a hood legend and

Ebony Chronicles of Elevation

all, but he had his run when Darnell was still a little shorty playing in the park. However, a half an hour ago he found himself waiting for the N40 bus to pick him up. Even at this very moment, he wondered why he had made the trip.

"Grab a seat. Stay a while," Walter said with a slight grin.

Darnell sat across from Walter on the opposite side of the table.

"So, if I recall, the last thing you asked me was how Marvin died, right?"

Darnell nodded his head while looking into Walter's face.

"Do you live with your father?" Walter asked.

"No."

"Do you know him?"

"No," Darnell replied again, wondering how this conversation suddenly became focused on him.

"I didn't know my father either. I heard about him from older people in my neighborhood though. They said he was a pimp...a lady's man. I guess that's why I was always good with the females," Walter said, pausing to chuckle to his self. "I never met him though, and that pissed me off because it made me feel worthless in a sense. Like, how could my own father not want to see me? My mother was always there, but still I had that void...that emptiness. You know what I mean?"

Darnell nodded his head.

Walter sipped from his green tea and continued saying, "That made me cold in a sense. I didn't really have feelings for anyone else, because if you feel worthless, how can you place value on another person? So, I lived my life kind of reckless when I was younger. I used to rob and steal and the whole nine. I never cared about anybody, including the women I used to lay up with. They were just jump offs, like you kids call them today."

88

The last comment brought a smile to Darnell's face.

"But, when my son was born, it changed me. I had actually created a life. At that point, I promised to be a better father than my own father had been to me," Walter said, leaving an awkward pause after his last statement.

"Were you?" Darnell asked.

"Yeah, definitely. I saw my son. I was a part of his life," Walter added, pausing again.

The uncomfortable silence caused Darnell to say, "But?"

"But, just because I was a better father than the one I had, doesn't mean I was a good father," Walter stated, this time pausing but continuing with his thought. "I saw Marvin every week or so and bought him things, but I didn't teach him any values. He saw the lifestyle I led and tried to emulate it. That's what sons do. I treated his mother like trash, so he treated women like trash. I hustled and was always involved in some kind of quick money scheme, so that's what he learned to do. I was a father, but I was no kind of mentor or role model. I let the streets raise him, and the streets don't care about no one."

There was pain etched across Walter's face which Darnell could not only see, but he could feel. The man across from him had lived a life filled with torment and regret. When Darnell peered at him, he saw all of these things, but he also saw himself. The pain he described from not knowing his father was one he knew all too well. The lack of respect he had for others and the feeling of worthlessness also resonated with him.

He thought about Mega, and then he thought about Demontay. He wondered how much his own son was observing and how much he was taking in. All of these things were clouding his mind with thoughts he didn't want to come to terms with or even attempt to understand at the moment.

Ebony Chronicles of Elevation

"You told me that Marvin was thorough. That's a term I hear you young cats use a lot. But, thorough means complete. How can you be complete if you're living a life that is void of values and morals? How can you be thorough if you don't have a father around to teach you any better?"

Darnell was unresponsive, his eyes becoming glassy as he stared blankly into nothingness.

"The last time I saw Marvin, I told him about legacy. We all have a purpose to build upon what our ancestors did before us. It's not enough to say I didn't know or to settle and not do better, just because someone didn't do better by us. It's up to us to make a difference. We have to—"

Darnell interrupted Walter by standing up. Stone faced he said, "I have to go."

Frown lines in Walter's forehead formed as he replied, "You just got here. I have so much more to tell you."

"I gotta go," Darnell said, before abruptly standing up and walking away from the table.

"I'll be here tomorrow," Walter yelled out. His words chased behind Darnell, but he wasn't sure if they caught his young companion's ears as he quickly fled from the cafe.

Chapter 13

Latrice Wilson was a petite, young, dark complexioned sister who lived in a small apartment on Terrace Avenue in Hempstead. She was only eighteen, but birthed two children already, with another on the way and no desire or motivation to do much of anything with her life. She had a twin sister named Latrell. They were identical in every manner, except their drive, determination and values.

They grew up in the same household, but Latrell aspired to go to college from a young age. She always excelled in school. When Latrice was out partying, she was in the house studying. The only thing the two had in common was their good looks.

Latrell had attempted on many occasions to convince her sister to go to cosmetology school, but Latrice always refused. She had the talent and ability to braid hair in any style and even taught herself how to do acrylic nails, but was never motivated to get her license so she could work in a shop. Instead, she was known as the one to see when you needed your hair "did" in the hood.

Today was no different. Latrice was sitting on the couch in her cluttered living room, watching paternity tests being done on Maury, while her own kids were causing a ruckus in the bedroom. A young hood named Sham's head was resting between her legs, while she used a small toothed comb and her fingers to give him tight box braids.

"That is not the daddy," Latrice yelled aloud with Maury. "I knew he wasn't. They ears and nose don't even look alike. These hoes out here are scandalous."

Sham didn't reply. He was young and soft spoken, which allowed him to blend in. People barely observed him, but he was very observant. He rarely wasted words and only spoke when the need arose.

"So, what's been good with you, Ma? It looks like your belly ready to pop," Sham said.

"I'm ready. The baby supposed to be here any day now," Latrice replied as she finished another braid.

"You sure know how to make some pretty babies. Every last one of them look just like you."

Latrice blushed. "You always know what to say, Sham. If you wasn't so young, I'd let you be one of my baby daddies."

Ebony Chronicles of Elevation

They both laughed aloud. Then Sham interjected by asking, "Who's the father of this one?"

"You don't know? It's your man."

"Who?"

"Buddy."

"Say word?"

"I said it. It's his, but he gonna mess around and make me take him to Maury."

"Why, he denying it?"

"Is he? I mean, he come around here and stuff, but it ain't to talk about his child. He just be trying to sweet talk me so I can give him information about my sister and the bank."

A perplexed expression came over Sham's face. "What bank?"

Latrice hesitated, realizing that she had said too much. Her hesitancy subsided when she realized that she was only talking to Sham, and he rarely spoke at all.

"Buddy and them is going to rob that Chase in Uniondale next Wednesday. That's when they'll have the most money there. You know, my old stuck up sister work there. Buddy been asking me all these questions about the bank, when he need to be telling me how much of that money he gonna give me to take care of our baby."

Sham remained silent, making mental notes as he took everything in. He was a master conversationalist, knowing when to talk and knowing when to listen. He knew when to prod and when to ease back as well. After waiting a few moments, he said, "Buddy is my man, but I can't believe you're having his baby though. Even still, he should be more concerned about you and his child on the way."

"That's what I'm sayin," Latrice replied.

"What type of questions has he been asking you about the bank?"

Chapter 14

For Darnell, the week had passed by in a weed induced blur. It seemed as if every day he was high or drunk, just to dull the pain he refused to deal with. Shalonda had been blowing up his Sidekick with text messages he didn't read and voicemail messages he refused to listen to. He didn't want to hear her voice, or the badgering and bickering that would accompany it.

This morning, he woke up with a bad premonition. It was like God was speaking to him, and he had never even been to a church except for funerals in the past. However, something had touched him and nudged him out of his drunken slumber. And while Buddy and Bam remained in a comatose state in the living room of Buddy's small apartment, he stared at himself in a small mirror in the bathroom, looking deep into his own soul.

The past week was spent going over the plan for the robbery, but every one of those days his mind had been clouded with thoughts of his last discussion with Walter Givens. He thought about things he wasn't comfortable thinking about, and wounds were uncovered that had been bandaged for several years.

When Darnell left the apartment, it was nearly noon and his friends were still asleep. He'd been in the bathroom since he had awakened, close enough to the toilet to vomit and within inches of the mirror to his soul. He stumbled out onto the street nursing a hangover, but determined to make it to the African American Museum.

Sun rays irritated his eyes, causing him to squint with each step he took toward the bus stop. He moved with motivation, and profound purpose. The stop where he caught the N40 was on Greenwich Street. It usually ran every forty minutes or so. When he reached Nassau Road, he saw a vision in the distance. It appeared next to the bus

Ebony Chronicles of Elevation

stop, sort of like a mirage. He wondered if his eyes were playing tricks on him.

As Darnell continued walking, he realized that he hadn't been hallucinating. The closer he got to the bus stop, the more he realized that the figure he observed from afar was indeed his mother. His eyes had not deceived him. However, it was no wonder why he had questioned whether it was his mother he had observed. She was wearing a dress and her hair was done. Today, she looked better than she had in years.

"Hi, Sheila," Darnell said, for the first time noticing the sadness in her eyes.

"Hi," she replied in a tone both cold and unfeeling. No matter how high, depressed or zoned out she was in the past, his mother always managed to exhibit some degree of excitement when she saw him. Today there was no light in her eyes.

"What's good? Why do you look Ike that?"

"No reason," Sheila replied, as she looked downward. She never looked Darnell in the eyes when they spoke, either from shame or guilt.

Words never came easy for either of them. They struggled to figure out what to say to one another and never were quite sure what to do.

"Where are you headed?" Darnell asked, eyeing an approaching transit bus in the near distance.

Her words came out hesitantly, as she chose them carefully. "I have to go to a funeral for an old friend of mines. What about you?"

"I'm going to see one of my boys."

"Well, you be careful. You know I be hearing stories about you and them streets. You don't want to end up like your father."

A bus heading toward Roosevelt pulled up. Darnell thought to ask about his father, but he had asked before and always got the same answers. His father was a thug; an OG, who had been in and out of prison his whole life before his untimely death.

The doors to the bus opened and a few passengers descended the steps as they departed. As she boarded the bus, Sheila glanced back at Darnell, for the first time looking into his face. Darnell looked at her, and then past his mother, seeing the bus driver who was waiting impatiently.

"I love you, Darnell," Sheila said.

"I love you too," Darnell replied, in a voice that sounded younger than he was.

Sheila walked up the steps and the doors to the bus closed behind her. Her son's eyes followed her the whole way. As the vehicle pulled away from the curb, Darnell thought back to when his mother used to say those three words to him all the time. That was before the alcohol, the cocaine and the addiction.

Thoughts still lingered in his mind as he crossed the street and waited for the bus that would be taking him in the opposite direction toward Hempstead. His mind had been so clouded that he had to remind himself to be conscious of his surroundings. He was on the battlefield, traveling through a warzone with danger lingering around every corner.

When his bus arrived, he quickly boarded it and sat all the way in the back, mindfully aware of everyone and everything. He thought about his father, visualizing what he might look like in his mind. He wondered how or if things would have been different, if they had actually known each other.

His bus ride was over before he knew it. After pulling into the bus terminal, he departed and headed a few blocks away to the African American museum. Today he felt more eager than ever to speak to Walter Givens. The little tidbits

Ebony Chronicles of Elevation

of knowledge and wisdom the old man shared with him, made him feel special. And while it forced him to think about uncomfortable periods in his own life, it was an exercise he needed to go through. It forced him to look directly in the mirror at himself.

Darnell entered the museum and walked toward the cashier who collected the admission fees at the front door. Knowing who he was, she hadn't asked for him to pay last time, but Darnell had his two dollars in hand just in case.

"Good afternoon," the young lady politely said. She had a peculiar expression on her face, which he picked up on immediately.

"Good afternoon," Darnell replied.

"Are you here to see the museum?"

Darnell held out the two-dollar admission fee and said, "No, I'm here to meet someone in the cafe."

The young lady maintained the same curious glare as she asked, "Is it Mr. Givens?"

"Yes," Darnell replied, wanting to say, "You know who it is."

The young girl's face saddened as she said, "You haven't heard the news?"

"What news?"

"Mr. Givens died this past weekend."

The words that followed didn't even register. Darnell asked what happened, but he didn't hear the reply. She told him that it was of natural causes, but when she explained that he had been battling cancer for some time now he had already tuned her out. She handed him an envelope that Mr. Givens had left for him last week, but he didn't realize what he was clutching in his hand until he was back on the bus and headed home. It was then that he finally got his thoughts around everything that had transpired and built up the courage to open the letter that read:

96

"I was hoping you would come back today, but I guess our last discussion was too deep. I was like you once, finding myself running away from my issues instead of dealing with them like a man. In any event, I want you to know a few things. We can't change the past, but we can control the choices we make in the future. It's not enough to just be better than the men that raised us. We have to be the best we can be. It's not enough to just father a child, if we are not nurturing, developing and fathering that child..."

There were more words on the paper, but Darnell stopped reading. He crumpled the letter up and stuck it in his pocket. Various emotions came over him all at once. He felt confused, saddened and also abandoned. In addition, he was fearful for what tomorrow would bring. After days of planning, it was finally time for the bank heist to take place.

At the same time in Second Shiloh Baptist Church, the funeral service for Walter Givens had just finished, and the hundreds of people in attendance were gathered together in line as they walked past the casket for a final viewing of the body. There wasn't a dry eye in the building, for the man that many had come to love and admire over the years.

Darnell's mother, Sheila was also in line. When she reached the area just in front of the pew, where the casket was, she closed her eyes and said a silent prayer. She was conscious of her appearance, and sort of shameful in a sense. The drugs had aged and decayed her, making her look nothing like her former self that many in attendance remembered her as. However, she would not have missed out on paying her final respects to a man who had helped her on more than one occasion over the years.

Sergeant Randy Ward also attended Walter's funeral. In his position as a Nassau County Police Officer for the past fifteen years, he had dealt with Walter on many

Ebony Chronicles of Elevation

occasions. Sergeant Ward had an impeccable record and an undeniable pulse for the streets. He was Caucasian, but he had the ability to converse effectively and appeal to the sensibilities of the blacks and Hispanics in the communities he served. Because of this, he had gained the trust of many individuals who wouldn't normally communicate with someone in law enforcement.

His list of confidential informants was extensive. They were mostly younger males or females in their mid to late teens. He liked them young because they were more in tune with what was going on. Also, it didn't take much to get information from them. Compensation was minimal, but the dividends were grandiose.

After viewing the body and bidding his final respects, Sergeant Ward left Second Shiloh Church quickly. He had to get to Hempstead for a meeting and he was already running late. Yesterday afternoon he received a call from a young informant he'd been working with named, Sham. Apparently, he had some information on the shooting and stabbing that took place at Taboo a few weeks ago, as well as an impending bank robbery happening tomorrow.

Chapter 15

Cardboard boxes cluttered the basement apartment, making it hard to move around in the confined space. It was Wednesday morning. Sun shined through the only windows allowing a peek outside, shedding light on this particular moment. Everything Shalonda owned was packed away and waiting on a u-Haul truck to arrive, so she could move back home with her parents. This was the result of an hour long phone call that took place two nights ago. It was a heart wrenching and humbling conversation that should have occurred more than five years-ago.

Demontay was fidgety and bored. Most of his toys were packed away and the cable television had been cut off. So, with nothing to do, he whined and complained asking, "When are we leaving?" over and over again. Shalonda tried to pacify him, but there was only so much she could do. Under the circumstances, she was also growing agitated by the minute. Finally, a knock at the basement door immediately lowered her stress level. With the movers arriving, she would begin her journey to an old place, but a new life.

She opened the door without looking out the window, unsuspecting but surprised when she saw who was waiting on the other side of the doorway. It was Darnell. They hadn't seen each other or spoken in well over a week. The bags under his eyes and ragged appearance made him look as if he hadn't slept much during that time period. He looked past Shalonda, noticing the boxes in the room. Then he noticed Demontay sitting on the floor at the same time his son noticed him.

"Daddy!" Demontay yelled, before running full speed and grabbing his father around the legs. If there was any apprehension Shalonda had about letting Darnell come inside, it quickly subsided as she watched her son's reaction.

Darnell picked Demontay up in his arms and stepped inside, before Shalonda closed the door behind him. His eyes scanned the room, already answering a question he felt compelled to ask. "Are ya'll moving?"

"Yes," Shalonda answered anticipating the next question before it was asked. "In with my parents."

"Are you coming with us, Daddy?" Demontay asked.

Darnell glanced at Shalonda. They stared in each other's faces for a brief moment before she looked away uncomfortably. Darnell put Demontay down on the floor

Ebony Chronicles of Elevation

and said, "Let me speak to your mother about it and I'll let you know, okay?"

Demontay replied, "Okay," before weaving between the boxes to retrieve the only toy that wasn't packed away.

"You got a minute to talk?" Darnell asked, noticing an immediate change in Shalonda's demeanor. "Look. I didn't come here to argue. I got some things on my mind that I need to talk to you about though."

"Okay, what is it?" Shalonda replied impatiently.

"I'm sorry," Darnell said.

In a sarcastic huff Shalonda replied, "Oh, here we go."

Darnell grabbed one of her arms lightly and said, "Just listen to me."

"Darnell, I already made up my mind. I can't live my life like this letting you hurt me. I don't deserve this and you don't deserve me. But, I'm not gonna be foul and try to keep you away from your son. However, I can't be with you no more. I just can't."

"But, I need you," Darnell replied softly as a tear rolled down his cheek.

She had never seen him cry before, and looking at him in this state sapped any will she had left in her to be defiant. "What's wrong, Darnell? You don't look like you've been sleeping and you're not acting like yourself. What's bothering you?"

"I just need you to know that I love you and I want to be with you. I know I've messed up in the past and I know you didn't deserve to be treated the way I treated you. You deserved better. I don't have no excuses, but all I can say is that I've been thinking a lot over the past few days and I want to make it better for us. I'm gonna make it better."

"Do you want to come move in with us?" Shalonda asked, surprising herself with her own words. "I can speak to my parents about it."

100

"Nah, I don't want you to speak to them. I gotta be a man and step up. I didn't even have the conversation I should have had with your father when I found out you were pregnant. I think I should speak to your parents myself."

A feeling of elation came over Shalonda. "So, you wanna move in with us?"

"I do, but I want to do things right. There's so much I gotta share with you. I don't want to just feed you a bunch of words though. I want to back them up with actions."

"The moving people will be here any minute. You can just ride over there with us now."

Darnell glanced to the spot on the wall where the clock used to be, then he looked back toward Shalonda and asked, "Do you know what time it is?"

"Eleven thirty."

"Okay. I gotta go handle something real quick, but I'll meet you at your parent's crib in a couple of hours," Darnell replied. He had a half an hour to get over to Buddy's apartment, where they'd be leaving from to do the robbery.

Shalonda grabbed his hand, immediately overwhelmed by a feeling of trepidation. "Please don't go. Nothing else could be as important as being with us right now."

"I don't want to see your parents like this. I'm just going to be a little while and then I'll meet you over there."

The eerie feeling continued to haunt her. As if on cue, Demontay ran over and hugged his father around the legs tightly. There were tears streaming down his face as he wrapped himself around Darnell's legs. "Don't go, Daddy."

"I have to go, but I'm gonna see you at Grandma and Grandpa's house."

Demontay maintained his grip and a smile came over his face. "You're moving with us?"

Ebony Chronicles of Elevation

"Yes," Darnell replied, mindful of the time and the fact that he had to leave quickly.

No relief came over Shalonda. Still holding onto Darnell's hand, she said, "Don't go out that door. I just have a bad feeling that if you leave, we're never gonna see you again."

A sarcastic grin came over Darnell's face. "Are you serious?"

"I just don't know what it is, Darnell, but I have a bad feeling. I'm begging you not to leave."

Darnell could barely conceal the fact that he had concerns as well, but he did his best to mask it. Instinctively, he knew she was right, but he had to go.

"Don't worry yourself. I just have to take care of one thing and I'll meet you over there."

The words were barely out of his mouth before a deluge of tears poured out of Shalonda's eyes. Darnell pulled her close to his chest and they cried together, both feeling as if it may be the last time they would be together.

Chapter 16

Wednesdays were the slowest day of the week at the Chase Bank located in Uniondale. Most of their patrons were paid on Thursdays or Fridays, when foot traffic was heaviest in and out of the bank. However, in preparation for the influx of people looking to cash their checks, a bank drop was made via armored car on Wednesdays. In essence, Wednesday was the day when most of the money was at the bank. The only people who knew this information were current employees, previous employees or those who knew either of the two.

Sergeant Ward and two dozen plain clothes police officers had been staking out the bank since it opened its doors, a little after eight o'clock this morning. They had officers on the sidewalk, in the parking lot and a few in the bank as well. Sergeant Ward even had a police officer who looked to be no older than nineteen posing as a new employee. Management at the bank agreed with that tactic, even encouraging the use of more police officers posing as bank tellers. However, Sergeant Ward refused, not wanting to tip anyone off if this was indeed an inside job.

It was a little after noon when Sergeant Ward noticed a suspicious looking vehicle pull into a municipal parking lot diagonally across the street from the bank. He was perched on the roof of a library which was right next door. Through binoculars with 12x zoom, he read the license plate number he saw into his walkie-talkie, verifying that the plates belonged to an Acura and not the Cavalier they were affixed to. That confirmed that the car was stolen, but just before twelve-thirty was when he confirmed that these were indeed his would be bank robbers.

That was when the red armored truck pulled in front of the bank and the stolen Cavalier slowly made its way out of the parking lot across the street before parking a car's length behind the armored vehicle. They were going to pull an outside job, which was smart. That meant there was less chance of people getting hurt or hostages being taken. Sergeant Ward exhaled a breath of relief.

The armored truck drivers were also police officers, who were swapped out earlier this morning. They sat behind the protective bulletproof glass, passively waiting before exiting the vehicle, confirming that everyone was in place by walkie-talkie. After receiving confirmation for the go ahead, an officer exited the driver's side of the vehicle wearing an All-Safe security uniform. He had his gun holstered as he walked to the rear of the truck surveying the area with each step. Once he reached the back of the truck he knocked twice before the locks could be heard disengaging. Then a security guard clutching an AK-47

Ebony Chronicles of Elevation

assault rifle hopped out of the vehicle, followed by another undercover officer who was holding a bulky money bag in each hand.

Overcast formed in the skies, hiding the sun as Sergeant Ward intently looked on. He was waiting for someone from the car to make a move so his officers could swoop in. This would be their best opportunity to intervene with little to no casualties. But, no one had done so much as opening a car door, which confused Ward. He wondered if somehow they had been spooked or tipped off.

The next action was unanticipated and unimaginable. With all his attention on the stolen car, Sergeant Ward had failed to notice another vehicle that pulled up and parked just around the corner from the bank minutes earlier. It was out of his viewpoint. Before he could see the lone gunman who had exited the vehicle, he heard a rapid release of gunfire from a high caliber weapon. Then he heard a crackling sound emit from his walkie-talkie, before someone yelled out, "Officer down! Officer down!" The sound of more gunfire could be heard followed by loud screams.

A few seconds later, Sergeant Ward finally saw movement from the stolen car. The passenger's door opened, before another gunman stepped out onto the sidewalk and begin firing a Tec-9 submachine gun in sporadic bursts. He provided cover fire as the masked gunman who had shot the police officers walking into the bank, ran toward the back of the car clutching the two bulky bags in his hands. He just reached the back door when gunfire erupted from all directions, ripping through the bodies of both men who were standing outside of the car.

The getaway driver slammed down on the gas, plowing over a fleeing pedestrian as he pulled away from the curb, gunning the car southbound on Uniondale

Avenue. He barely made it to the corner before marksmen posted on the roof of a strip mall on the adjacent block sent a bullet through his ski mask that exploded in his brain. The car swerved across the yellow lines dividing the street before crashing into a chain link fence in front of a real estate office.

Chapter 17

A week had passed since the failed bank robbery, but it was still on a lot of people's minds. The news had run a story each day, questioning whether excessive force was used by the police officers. Fortunately, no officers had died, each survivor suffering extensive wounds. However, all three robbers were pronounced dead at the scene. Civil rights leaders were demanding an investigation, although they couldn't dispute the fact that the young men in question had shady pasts and a history of violence.

Hand in hand, Shalonda and Demontay walked down the gravelly pathway at the Greenfield Cemetery. It was located right around the corner from where she used to live, but this was the first time she had ever been inside. Darnell never liked the burial place, which added a bit of irony to the whole situation, being that they were coming here to see him. Shalonda walked quietly, only talking to answer the inquisitive questions coming from her son.

When they reached the tombstone, Shalonda pulled a paper from her pocket. The ground was still exposed in front of the tombstone and the grass had yet to grow. Several bouquets of flowers were posted around the grave, their scent still fresh and aromatic in the immediate area. Shalonda unfolded the crumpled paper she held in her hand as Demontay looked up at her. This was the first time she had actually read the words that were printed in fine black ink. The letter read:

Ebony Chronicles of Elevation

"I was hoping you would come back today, but I guess our last discussion was too deep. I was like you once, finding myself running away from my issues instead of dealing with them like a man. In any event, I want you to know a few things. We can't change the past, but we can control the choices we make in the future. It's not enough to just be better than the men that raised us. We have to be the best we can be. It's not enough to just father a child, if we are not nurturing, developing and fathering that child. The only way we break the cycle that is paralyzing our race is by being open and honest with ourselves. What type of men are we if we are merely repeating the wrongs that have been done to us?

The night that we "met", I saw something in your eyes. There was fear like I said, but also a familiarity. Like my own son, somebody failed you. They didn't teach you how to be a man, but that does not mean you can't learn how to be one. I failed my son and because of that he failed his son, it's up to you to break the cycle. The familiarity I saw in your eyes is one that only a grandfather would know. I saw Marvin when I looked in your face that night and I knew immediately that you were Sheila's son, my grandson. My only hope now is that we have the opportunity to get to know each other better, because I only have a little time left. But even if we never see each other again, you have to promise to be more of a man than I was. For our legacy is not determined by what we've done for us, but what we do for those who will continue to live on after us.

With Love,

Walter Givens

A single tear rolled down Shalonda's face as she looked at the name on the tombstone. Then she glanced down at her son who was playing with some rocks on the ground, oblivious to what was going on. He looked so much like his father that it was impossible for you to see one and not think of the other.

Just then, a figure walked up slowly from behind, startling Shalonda slightly.

"Did you read it?" he asked.

"Yeah."

"Do you understand now?"

"Yes, I do."

Demontay leaped from the ground and wrapped his arms around his father's legs, a wide smile immediately coming across his face. It was the same way he had clung on to Darnell's legs the day of the botched robbery. That was the day he finally became a man, choosing his family over his "friends". Choosing not to meet Buddy at his apartment that afternoon.

"Unknowingly, I spared my grandfather's life and unselfishly he saved mine, so I could save his," Darnell stated as he grabbed his son beneath his under arms and held him high in the air.

Looking toward Shalonda, Darnell said, "I hope you understand now. I hope you believe me when I say that I promise to be a better man and a better father."

"I do, baby. And I love you."

"I love you too," Darnell stated before glancing upward into his son's eyes and saying. "It's time to break the cycle."

Facebook Friends

Q.B. Wells

Part 1
Cheaters

Midnight in the Chicago suburb of Niles, a half burned yellow, sky blue and black Bahamian flag flung outside the porch of a three door, two story house. The fringes of the flag had turned brown as yellow snow below had stained. Somebody urinated below the flag and the burned ashes around the six inches of snow resembled an erupted volcano.

Lashaunda Vallejo called the Niles police the day before. Her hands trembled as she showed the officer the flag and she pleaded when she told him she thought the burned flag was a hate crime. She was the only black person in the neighborhood and the only family with a mixed daughter, "Somebody pissed right here on my porch officer, what would you think if it was your family?

"I would think that some kids were playing around and maybe took the joke too far," replied the police officer. He made a report and left the matter alone. Nobody needed the extra trouble.

Lashaunda Vallejo couldn't leave the matter alone. She didn't know what was going on. Her husband Tony was away on business more than ever. She knew something was wrong and she didn't know what to think about the incident, the neighborhood or even her marriage. The world was against her and her life felt like a bed of lies.

For the past years she spent life at home caring for their daughter until she was old enough to graduate high school. She exchanged the years of taking care of her daughter for years and years of professional experience. Now she was behind in work experience and looking for a way to gain her own identity and independence in life. Her daughter was away at college and she felt the need to show an example.

She skimmed through the Facebook friends of her old classmates as she lay in her bedroom with the door half-open. Her husband Tony laid asleep downstairs in the basement. Lashaunda had spent the last four hours on Facebook, reminiscing about old high school flings. She scrolled Facebook for her favorite high school sweetheart, Dexter. She had searched for his name for months and was surprised to finally find him. She wasn't sure if she should request a friendship. She had already befriended his wife.

She remembered two things about Dexter. A dude clowned him in class because he took the short yellow bus to school. Dexter slammed him on his head in front of the class. The second detail she remembered was Dexter had a long penis, longer than anyone she had ever had. His thing would bulge through his pants when he sported sweatpants. A classmate wrestled with Dexter's snake one day after school and told her how long her pussy ached afterwards. Lashaunda was scared but curious to find out if the opportunity presented itself. Her mother had told her never to waste time on a penis smaller than a banana and she never disobeyed her Mother's advice.

Lashaunda was happy she listened. When Dexter's snake was erect and they had sex, he worked her so hard that she thought he was mad at her. She didn't want to have sex with anyone else. It would be a waste of time. The thought of how hard Dexter made her cum made Lashaunda shiver and contemplate more about being his Facebook friend.

Ebony Chronicles of Elevation

The problem was Dexter couldn't keep his penis in his pants. He drove young girls and grown women wild. As she scrolled down the blue screen of profile faces, she wouldn't have been surprised if Dexter was online soliciting sex. She would pay for a day or two even if she had to take the cash off her husband's credit card. Men like Dexter were hard to find.

In high school, girls fought over him. A few girls settled for the fact that Dexter would just sex other women. Lashaunda unknowingly did that too. She dated Dexter for a year before she learned about his cheating. She had been walking down the hallway at school, when suddenly it felt like a truck had smashed into the back of her head. She had fallen to the ground, and she felt like hot water dripped down the back of her head and down her back.

"Bitch! You fuck with my man again and I'll cut you," a voice shouted overhead.

Lashaunda's head lifted and then dropped back to the floor. She saw bright lights and felt like someone had sprinkled feathers in her eyes and mouth. A crowd of students encircled the nurse and security guards as they attended to Lashaunda. She laid in the middle of the hallway until the ambulance arrived.

At the hospital, she learned that she had been hit in the back of the head with a pair of brass knuckles, and that her hair had been cut and then thrown in her face.

The girl who hit her was Patrice Latimore. Patrice took the yellow bus to school with Dexter. She later had a child by Dexter, and they had been married for six years. Life had moved on since high school but the scars wouldn't let Lashaunda let go of her past.

I would kill that bitch if I saw her today. Lashaunda thought about getting back at Patrice in another way. Dexter had called Lashaunda for years after he moved in with Patrice. Lashaunda's pussy got moist just thinking about sex with Dexter, but she was smart enough to control her urges. She could have any man she wanted and few men had the opportunity to sniff her pussy—it was squeaky clean with low mileage. Any man who dated Lashaunda knew that she was a keeper. Everyone that is, except her husband, Tony. He walked to the door.

"What you doing, Honey?"

Lashaunda stood up, showing Tony her gleaming brown skin and nappy fro hair. She looked at Tony as she shifted her pick through her hair. "Why are you still here? I'm doing nothing; I'm looking for a friend on Facebook."

"Is it a male friend?"

"Damn Tony, why does it matter? We are separated and getting a divorce. I wish you would just move out, but you are too damn stubborn and cheap." She closed her gown, the nipples of her breast pressed through the robe. "Get out and go to your girlfriend's house."

Tony stepped into the room. "When will you realize that I made a mistake, Lashaunda? I don't want her—I want you, my wife."

"Bullshit. You should have thought about that before you fucked that bitch! Do you know how many offers I had from men to cheat? Even your so called friends. I was good to you. I thought you were different, Tony, but you aren't."

"I...."

"Get the hell out of my room. You stay in the basement until you get an apartment. Leave me the hell alone before I fuckin' kill you!" she screamed as she slammed the door.

Normally, Tony would have kicked in the door, but he felt so guilty that he shuffled back down to the basement. He would get her back in another way.

Lashaunda despised every second that Tony was still in the house. If he wasn't gone in two days, she would get him out one way or another. If it were legal, she would cut

Ebony Chronicles of Elevation

his balls off and throw them down the drain for having his affair.

Instead, she decided to find a way to provide for her daughter and herself.

Tony would have to pay child support and the house payments after the divorce, he had stopped paying for anything the minute she said that she wanted the divorce. Once the court made him pay, the alimony and house payments wouldn't be enough to support her lifestyle or the college tuition for her daughter.

Lashaunda slept fitfully. She couldn't sleep. Her past haunted her. What would have happened if she had never been hit in the head with Patrice's brass knuckles? After the incident, Lashaunda's parents moved her from the public school to an all-girl Catholic School called St. Ignatius. The girls at the mostly white school teased her about her Bahamian accent. They teased her so much that she practiced for a year to make her accent go away. It seemed the moment she got rid of her accent, she gained more friends and a St. Ignatius friend introduced her to an Italian boy, Tony. They spent a summer together, went to prom and eventually got married.

Tony was nerdy and safe, like the opposite of everything that she was afraid of in Dexter. He was short and had dark brown hair. She liked him as much for his character as for his family upbringing. His father owned a construction business, and after Tony finished school, his family's plan was for him to take over the business. His wife was destined to have babies and stay at home.

That would have been the plan if Lashaunda was white. Once Tony's parents learned that their son was marrying a black woman, they insisted that she work. She needed to prove she was not lazy. Lashaunda refused to talk to them after the wedding and the stress had caused her to drink and plot-two things she had never experienced before the marriage.

Lashaunda was tall; her legs were long and dark. At the wedding, the families sat on separate sides of the aisle. They didn't talk at the reception, or even afterward. Lashaunda felt like it was her and Tony against the world, but she thought things might change when she had their daughter, Angela. Instead, things got worse with his family, and Tony increasingly stayed away from home.

Four years later, Lashaunda felt more alone than ever. She and Angela stayed in the four bedroom house in the Niles. There wasn't a black face to be found except herself and the creamed-coffee color of her daughter's skin.

Angela was her only family, and Lashaunda had to do something to secure their future. She had nothing to her name except an insurance policy and a .38 pistol that Tony had bought for her to protect herself while he was away.

Tony had taken her to the shooting range to show her how to use the gun. If she had known he was cheating, she would have shot him right then. After all, the last time she'd been cheated on, she'd ended up in the hospital. As far as Lashaunda was concerned, letting a cheating man live might just be her own death sentence. "Tony put my life—my daughter's life—in danger", Lashaunda thought. She was only able to sleep once she conjured a solution to clean the stain of her husband's last name.

Part II
Snapped

The light of morning brightened the room as Lashaunda stood up. She felt brand new and free for the first time in years. Tony had felt so guilty that he left early in the morning, and Lashaunda had the house to herself.

Ebony Chronicles of Elevation

She knew that Tony was gone, or she would have felt his bad vibes radiating through their house. She smiled, excited with the possibilities of the day. She gathered some clothes and placed them in the basket for the wash, and then walked down the stairs. Lashaunda sniffed and frowned. She had expected to smell the fragrance of an open, airy space, but instead was hit with the scent of perfume.

She didn't wear the perfume.

She paced until she determined the fragrance was coming from the basement. She carried the basket of clothes down to the basement and into the laundry room. The perfume smell was strongest in the laundry room. As she placed the clothes in the washer, she pondered why the smell was so strong in there. She searched beneath the sink and behind the washer. Could he have been so sloppy drunk that he got bolder than she ever thought he would? She couldn't find any other evidence other than the smell of another woman.

She had to get Tony out the house. She hummed to herself as she thought of her plot. Then she felt the urge, and ran to the bathroom to relieve herself. When she lifted the toilet lid, a condom floated in the water. Who the fuck does he think he is?

Piss poured out like a raging bull. Tony must think she was some dumb bitch. He really thought she was stupid. Lashaunda slammed the toilet lid down and charged up the stairs. For years she stayed at home taking care of their child. Now the child was a teenager away at college. She had done a great job raising her-mostly alone. Tony stayed away at work, hardly showing an interest in her. Lashaunda had sacrificed time to nurture her family in the way that Tony expected. She had turned down a job in the largest black advertising agency in Chicago because she thought it was her duty to take care of her family. Now with her daughter away at college, she couldn't have better timing.

She gagged at the thought of some woman fucking her husband in her house. The white boy had shitted on her for the last time! After all the trips to Rome and the five bedroom house in the suburbs and the car he had given her, she didn't step out on him. She wanted to, but she believed Tony when he said no white or black man would want her.

Lashaunda believed that the tall, dark black men she was attracted to didn't have jobs. Men she liked had been to jail, had too many kids or cheated on their women. She believed it all and there was no way she could find a quality black man. Lashaunda was afraid to date a black man, because she knew that he would do her wrong like Dexter. Even worse, she might have to deal with some baby momma trying to shoot her, slice her face or throw bleach in her face.

As the condom floated in the toilet, she realized that she had married Tony because she loved him. She loved him because he was honest, hardworking and safe. He opened doors and sponsored her. Tony would be faithful and keep out of trouble. Instead, for years he had luxurious affairs while she stayed at home without hardly any contact with friends or family.

Tony had used her because she was too assuming. She trusted too much. She would not her trust get in the way.

Lashaunda avoided confrontation in the past. She grew up a foster child in Skokie, Illinois, but went to high school on the north side of Chicago. After the assault, she moved back to Niles and attended college at Loyola University. Now, Lashaunda lived even farther away from Chicago and the artsy vibes that made her fall in love with the City.

Ebony Chronicles of Elevation

She had to do something different, or people would continue to mistreat her. She walked back downstairs to the floating condom. Her first thought was to keep the condom for evidence, but then she flushed it down the toilet with a slam of her fist against the lever.

She stormed upstairs and grabbed her laptop, then took it down to the kitchen and logged into Facebook. She already had five inbox messages from men soliciting sex. All the men were strays, and they might not even be good in bed. She didn't have the time or the inclination to waste her time with bad sex. She'd had enough of that from her husband.

She wanted to cum hard, not on the bed but on top of the kitchen counter, the dining room table or on some man's mustache. She wanted to cum in somebody's mouth. She wanted Dexter. She went to his wife's profile page and found his profile under Patrice's list of friends.

Dexter looked damn good she thought. He was an ex-wrestler and had been keeping in shape. At forty-two years old, he still had a six-pack. His profile picture was of him in the gym with a tank top and a baseball hat on. He was dark and had wavy hair with a little gray. What a ho, Lashaunda thought. His relationship status was not included in his profile info but she knew he was still married.

She sent him a friend request. Her first urge was to send him a message about old times. There were many good memories. They had broken two beds during their relationship. He was the first man who licked her clit until her legs shook and she squirted cum all over his face.

She was still classy. Even though she wanted to get even with her husband, she didn't want Dexter to think about how she had changed. Her sex life had plummeted since she and Dexter had broken up, and she yearned to get that old feeling back. At least once, possibly twice.

Before she could remember the last time they fucked, Dexter accepted her friend request. He sent a message to her inbox, too.

Hey Sexy, I've been looking for you for years! Give me a call 443.500.0990.

Dexter

Lashaunda felt giddy as a teenager. He had been looking for her! She didn't want to call too soon, but she had to. Tony would be home by 5 p.m.

She stopped thinking and called Dexter.

"Hello," he answered.

"Hey stranger," she purred.

"Stranger? You the one that hasn't returned my calls and then moved out to Never Never Land with that old white man."

"Whatever."

"Is he treating you right?"

"Nope, not at all," Lashaunda confessed. With anyone else she would have kept the information a secret, but she felt comfortable talking with Dexter, even after all the time that had passed. He was one of the only men she had been with.

"Well, at least you have the big house in the hills, with a gate," said Dexter. "It could be worse."

"I guess so. It could be better. Life wouldn't have been no better with you. You would have had half the town pregnant!" she said, laughing. "It's because of you that I'm traumatized."

"I traumatized you? I bet you miss me, though," he said. Dexter thought that every girl he had sex with wanted to go another round.

"Boy, you crazy!"

"I'm crazy, but you too. Can I come see you?"

"I have a husband, Dexter," said Lashaunda.

Ebony Chronicles of Elevation

"He don't treat you right. You just said he didn't. We can just talk."

Lashaunda paused. "Don't you have a wife or a girlfriend?"

"Nope. I had a girl I was seeing, but she's not like you. Why don't you come out here and get me?"

"Come get you. You don't have a car?"

"Not right now, it's a long story. We'll talk about it when you get here."

"I'm not coming."

"Why not?"

"I might get lost. I will take you back, but you will have to find your way here if you want to see me."

"Okay, I'll be there in an hour," Dexter said.

Lashaunda hung up, and then tapped her fingernails on the counter. She hoped he would find the way to her home soon. It was already past noon. She went downstairs and slipped on some tight jeans and a fitted shirt. The house was chilly, so she put on her robe. Then she peeked out the side of the front window curtain, mesmerized by the rain drizzling down on the hood of her car.

Something in her was afraid, but she was excited at the same time. She had never cheated before, or even thought about it. Years of putting her family first had her feeling like she was two steps behind life. She had always put herself last. Now she was going to do something for her and nobody else.

Lashuanda's heart raced when she heard the knock on the door. She tossed off the robe and waited a few minutes, until the knock came again. "I'm coming," she yelled, as if she hadn't heard the knock first. She opened the door.

"Wow, Lashaunda, you look good," Dexter replied. He stood at the door, looking stunned like he couldn't move.

"Are you going to come in out the rain or just stand there?"

"You have a banging house out here, too. Took a little longer than I thought to get here."

"I see. I'm just glad you could finally make it." She stood up straight so he could see her shape as they walked down the front hall. "Would you like something to drink?"

"Yeah, I'll take a Crown Royal."

"Dang, Dexter, I meant some water or juice or something. You want some alcohol!"

"Hell yeah, give me whatever you got. It's been a rough afternoon and I need to take off the edge."

Lashuanda reached into the cabinet and pulled out a bottle of scotch. She poured two shots and walked over to Dexter.

Dexter laughed. "First you talking about me drinking, then you bring me two drinks. You trying to get me drunk?"

"One of these shots is for me. You not the only one that's going to get they drink on."

The scotch burned Lashaunda's chest, but after it went down she felt easier about the decision she had made. Dexter was just as tall as she remembered, and his arms were thick. His lips were full and his eyes carried a curious wonder. Lashaunda had always loved his muscles. He wore a soft muscle shirt that she wanted to rip off of him, but instead she let him talk. For fifteen minutes, Dexter talked so much and so fast that he could have been speaking Chinese for all she knew.

Her panties soaked as she waited for Dexter to get it together. She didn't want to talk, she wanted to fuck. Then, finally he said the words she was waiting to hear.

"You want to go upstairs?"

"I thought you were never going to ask. No, I don't want to go upstairs, I want to do you right here, right now."

Ebony Chronicles of Elevation

Part III
Dumb and Dumber

Dexter watched Lashaunda pull off her shirt, glad to see that his trip was well worth the effort. He had stood up his buddy for drinks and borrowed ten bucks to take a cab that he'd ditched two blocks away from Lashaunda's house.

Lashuanda's nipples were large as quarters; her stomach was flat. She was fine. She was the finest woman he'd ever had the chance to fuck. He had truly missed her in their years apart.

Now that he had nothing to his name, he was going to beat her vagina like she owed him something. He had to be better than anything she'd ever had—his life depended on it. He had been kicked out of the house, lost his job, and everyone he knew was sure he was a failure. Lashaunda had her big house, her Lexus truck, and good intentions—she was his best prospect. She was the last remaining person who would see him in a positive light. He would make the most of it—he would make her cum so hard she'd be willing to do anything he wanted.

Dexter's bulge pressed against his jeans so hard that it hurt. Lashuanda observed, and dropped her pants at the sight. She posted on all fours on the couch. Dexter paced over to her and stripped down his pants. He braced himself behind her, opened the lips of her pussy and padded her clit with his dick.

She moaned loud. After a minute, Dexter bent down, peeled the lips back again, and licked the clit slowly from the back. Next he moved to her ass and licked her rectum till the pussy and ass shined. She squirted cum on his face, grabbing his face from behind. Lashaunda's leg shook and cum dripped down her legs as he jammed his thumb into her rectum. Cum dripped to his fingers and mouth. She was shook already—and he hadn't even put his dick in yet.

Lashaunda looked at her watch.

"Now, let's go upstairs," she said. She gathered her clothes and rushed up to the bedroom.

Dexter's dick was thick and heavy—he was ready now, more than ever. He ran up the stairs and found Lashaunda on her bed with her legs spread wide open. He tossed his clothes to the ground.

"You want this pussy?"

"Yeah I want that pussy."

"Come get it then. Come get this wet pussy."

Dexter jumped to the challenge. He straddled Lashaunda and fiddled her vagina with the head of his dick until she begged.

"Put it in me, put it in me now," Lashaunda murmured with ecstasy. She wrapped her feet around his middle and pulled his ass till she took all of him inside her.

Dexter couldn't play any longer. He went to work, slapping her ass and pounding until she yelled and grabbed a handful of his hair.

Lashaunda screamed her last orgasm. Dexter pulled out and shoved her onto her stomach. He shot a load of cum beside her.

They lay in the bed, silent, both enjoying the moment of their bodies. Dexter wanted to go another round, but when he rolled over, Lashaunda was asleep. The scotch and the hard work had made him a little woozy, and he hadn't been in a warm, comfortable bed in months. Soon, Dexter was asleep.

Lashaunda jerked awake when Tony opened the front door to the house and called, "Lashaunda, come here! I have something to show you."

Dexter woke up to find Lashaunda jumping into her fitted pants like a rabbit. She threw on her shirt. "My

Ebony Chronicles of Elevation

husband is home early," she tossed him his clothes. "Get into the closet until I can slip you out."

Dexter darted to the closet with his rear out. He put on his clothes as she left the room. There was no time to ask questions. Nor did he care if he had to hide in the closet. It was warm and cozy compared to the rain outside. As long as he eventually got a ride or a few bucks for a taxi, he would be happy—he didn't intend to leave the house quietly if he had to fend for himself in that neighborhood. The police might stop him or a neighbor would call the police for a suspicious character. His jeans and hooded muscle shirt blended in when he was in his neighborhood, but up here he looked like a criminal.

After about thirty minutes, Dexter thought he couldn't stay in the closet too much longer. Due to a short stint in prison, he was claustrophobic. Sweat dripped from his forehead. He hadn't heard anything from Lashaunda since she left.

Dexter wondered what he would do if her husband came upstairs. He glanced around the closet, at the suits and the piles of small boxes. A cane lay in the corner. Dexter picked up the cane, just in case Lashaunda's spouse found him and wanted to act stupid.

Dexter heard yelling and fussing from downstairs. He opened the door to hear better. There was a scream. Dexter's eyes opened wide and he crept out of the closet. He stood in the doorway to the hall and strained his ears.

"I smell fuckin' cologne, Lashaunda. You had some man in my house?"

"No, Tony I know you had some bitch," she responded. "You just feel fucking guilty. I should have a man."

Dexter could hear the husband rummaging through closets and doors, then the soft thumping of Lashaunda's footsteps on the stairs. He rushed back to the closet as she reached the top of the stairs.

Lashaunda entered the room and closed the door. She headed for the closet.

The bedroom door flew open—Tony was behind. "If you weren't fucking in the house, then let me smell your pussy. Let me see how moist it is."

"Are you crazy? I can't believe you would even ask me something like that. I don't owe you any explanations, we are getting a—"

Tony grasped her neck before she could finish her sentence. "I've compromised, Lashaunda, don't you think?" he applied pressure and lifted her.

Lashaunda's feet left the floor. She gagged and her eyes rolled toward the back of her head.

Dexter watched, not knowing what to do. He thought he should jump out and help, but everything was happening so fast.

With all her might, Lashaunda kneed Tony in the stomach. He bent over in pain and she punched him while he was down. She darted for the door but was tripped. Tony hammered the back of her head with his fist. She lay still as he yanked the pants off her body. He opened his pants and took off his shirt, tossing it next to the closet.

Dexter rushed out of the closet with the cane and swinging it like a bat, knocked the man across the head as hard as he could. Afraid that Tony would get up and attack, Dexter hit him repeatedly until he forgot where he was and what he was doing. When Dexter came back to himself, Tony laid still below him. Lashaunda was nowhere in sight. Dexter wondered where she was—and then heard a gunshot.

"Ahh," Tony spasmed and squirmed on the ground. Dexter's eyes found Lashaunda, who stood across the room with a gun in her hands.

Ebony Chronicles of Elevation

"He's not dead," she said. Without another word, she shot a second bullet into her husband's abdomen.

Dexter didn't know what to do. The police would be coming soon. He just wanted to get some sex from a Facebook friend, and instead he found himself in the middle of a murder. He cried out, "What are we going to do? I can't go back to jail."

"Nothing," Lashaunda said. She dumped two bullets into Dexter's chest.

He flopped to the floor in wonder, not knowing why his old fling would shoot him. The last image he saw was of her dark shadow dashing away. The last sound he heard was, "Oh, hurry, my husband is dead!" The last feeling he had was Lashaunda lifting his hand and placing his finger on the trigger. He was too weak to resist and his hand fell limp as his life expired.

The police arrived and took Lashaunda to the station. They questioned her for hours. She told them that she had found her ex on Facebook and they had sex. Her jealous husband came home enraged after he had a hunch she had sex with another man in the house. They argued and Tony assaulted her as Dexter was in the closet. Dexter stormed out the closet with the cane. He beat Tony and thought he was dead but Tony was shifty and pulled out a gun. Tony and Dexter fought, struggled with the gun, and her husband shot Dexter. Lashauda grabbed her husband from behind and he dropped the gun. Injured but not dead, Dexter picked up the gun and shot and killed her husband before he too died. She told the police Dexter had been calling her for years. She had been lonely and afraid when her husband was away but they never had any other problems. She broke into tears.

The officer knew she had been through a lot for any person. The police let Lashaunda go, she had experienced enough bad times already. The double murder was an odd occurrence but she was not guilty.

Two weeks later, Lashaunda and her daughter went to pick up a check from the insurance company. Tears fell from behind her glasses as she signed the check and handed the pen to the agent.

"I'm sorry for your loss. I hope the policy is enough to take care of you and your daughter during this difficult time, Mrs. Vallejo."

"Nothing could replace our loss," said Lashaunda. She placed the envelope in her pocket and grasped her daughter's hand. Her daughter cried some but she held in tears to comfort her mother. Lashaunda did not need her comfort.

Lashaunda had secured the house and the lifestyle she desired—$1.5M in insurance. Enough to pay for the remainder of her daughter's college tuition. Single might not be so bad. Lashaunda had a whole life ahead to find herself. While hugging her daughter she took off her glasses and wiped her eyes. The snow had melted and the sun peaked from behind the clouds. No matter the weather Lashaunda's smile was brighter than it had been in years. She pulled down her shades, drove home and decided she would buy a new house and sell the old home before she reached her driveway.

She told no one of her plans.

Minutes after she walked into the house she walked back on the porch and replaced the burned cloth on the porch with a brand new Bahamian flag. She no longer cared about anyone in the neighborhood or what the world thought of her life. She knew she was not weak or stupid. She ended the baggage from her past and prayed none of her tactics would come back to haunt her. When she got home she deleted Patrice Latimore as her Facebook friend.

DOWN FALL

Eyone Williams

In the streets, every move could be your last. Endless plots against you, constant conflict, schemes for what you have—your money, your woman, your life. This is what the street guy faces every day. In the streets, you must identify your enemies quickly. Without doing so you cannot effectively defend yourself. You must, by all means, force them to show their true colors so that you can spot them from far away. Learn them by their moves, their ways, their speech and patterns. What they hold in their hearts is far worse than what comes out of their mouths. Identify them as quickly as you can.

CHAPTER 1

Keeping it 100, Chub would be lying if he said he wasn't paranoid. His heart was pounding in his chest and his palms were sweaty. Another dead giveaway was the way his eyes were darting all over the place as he came out of the stairwell in the back of a Northwest, Washington, D.C. apartment building. It was a little after two in the morning. Anything could go down in such places; in fact, Chub had seen it all go down in such places. Nevertheless, he was being extra careful this go 'round being as though he had his girl with him. His girl, Trina, was more than just a girlfriend. Trina was his partner in almost everything he had going on in the streets. They watched each other's backs. They took care of one another. They got money together and more. On top of all of that, they were in love. Tonight, they were being put to the test. As they exited an apartment on the third floor they noticed a dude with a baseball cap pulled down low over his eyes. They really couldn't see the dude's face but that caught their attention and put them on the defensive.

"What the fuck is up with this nigga, Chub?" Trina asked as she gripped her Gucci bag firmly, walking swiftly behind Chub.

"I don't know what the fuck is up with this joker." Chub said, looking over his shoulder, leading the way to the back door of the apartment building where their car was parked.

"Did you leave the pistol in the car?" Trina asked.

"Fuck yeah." Chub said, kicking himself in the ass mentally as they bent the corner.

Not far behind them the stairwell down opened and shut again. The dude with the baseball cap was still on their trail.

He was moving fast, like a man with a purpose. Thinking fast, Chub stopped dead in his tracks and spent around to face Trina. Looking her in the eyes, he said, "Get to the car, hurry up."

"What you 'bout to do." Trina asked with her eyebrows raised.

"I'm bout to see what's good with this nigga and I don't want you right here. Ain't no sense in lettin' him follow us to the alley."

"Okay," Trina said as she headed out the back door into the darkness of the early morning hours.

Ebony Chronicles of Elevation

Chub took a deep breath and stepped out of the door behind Trina, but instead of following her up the back steps to the alley he hid on the other side of the door. Seconds later, the dude with the baseball cap came out of the door with a pistol drawn. Giving the dude no time to react, Chub rocked him with a left hook that smashed into the dudes jaw. The dude took the punch well but still flew against the brick wall. Chub rushed him, grabbing for the pistol. The dude fought back. He wasn't trying to let Chub get the ups on him by taking his pistol.

In a life or death struggle for the pistol, Chub managed to grunt, "What the fuck is up?! Who sent you?!"

The dude with the baseball cap said nothing, only gave it his all to wrestle his pistol free.

Chub gave him a mean knee to the mid section that made the dude crumble to the ground. However, he kept his grip on his pistol. In fact, the closer Chub came to taking control of the gun the stronger the dude got. With one last thrust of force, Chub kneed the dude high and hard right in the mouth, knocking his two front teeth out. He snatched the pistol from the dude's hands and smacked him in the face with it.

With murder in his eyes, Chub put the pistol to the dude's head and hissed, "Who sent you? Who the fuck sent you?!"

The dude rolled over and balled up into a knot. He was defeated and was accepting whatever his fate was to be.

Chub kicked him in the stomach with all the force he could muster. The dude let out a painful grunt. "Who the fuck sent you?!" "He'll kill me!" the dude said.

"Who you gon' worry about? Me, the nigga wit' a gun in your face or some other nigga that sent you on a crash-dummy mission? If I was you I would start thinking real fast cause you got less than sixty seconds to start talkin'."

"I don't know who sent me!" the dude shouted.

Chub kicked him in the face, made him grunt in pain one more time. "Wrong fuckin' answer, nigga!"

"Fuck!" the dude shouted, holding his bloody mouth. "All I know is a nigga name Black sent me at you, said if I could snatch you he would give me five Gs. That's all I know, I swear to God, on my mother!"

Chub kicked him in the face again. "Fuck I look like? Huh? Do I look like I was born yesterday, nigga?!"

"Ah, shit!" the dude grunted. "That's all I know!"

"Chub!"

Chub looked over his shoulder and saw Trina standing at the top of the steps. "I told you to go get in the car."

"You was takin' too long, I thought—"

Before Trina could finish her sentence the dude with the baseball cap found the energy to rush Chub. He lunged for the gun.

BOOM! BOOM! BOOM!

Gunshots sounded off with a thunderous roar. Trina wanted to scream. She couldn't believe her eyes. Her mouth dropped open as she watched the body fall limp to the ground. Smoking gun in hand, Chub looked down at the dead body and couldn't believe his eyes. It all had happened so quickly.

Trina shook her head and said, "Come on, let's go. Let's get the fuck outta' here. Now!"

Chub slowly backed away from the dead body. Grabbing Trina by the hand he jogged to the car, looking around to see if there were any witnesses in sight. He sees no one, but he was sure the gunshots had grabbed someone's attention.

They wasted no time jumping in the car. Chub started the Charger and backed out of the parking space. "I

Ebony Chronicles of Elevation

don't know what the fuck that was all about, baby." Chub said as he bent the corner, flying up Aspen Street.

Looking over her shoulder to make sure no one was following them, Trina said, "I don't think nobody saw us."

"I hope not." Chub said as his mind raced. "That nigga back there said some nigga name Black sent him."

"Black? Black who? Who the fuck is Black?"

Shaking his head, Chub said, "I know a thousand Blacks. But I don't got no problems wit' none of them. It's more to that than the nigga would say before I popped his ass."

"We need to find out then." Trina said as she looked at the duffle bag in the back seat.

"Trust and believe I'm gon' find out, sooner than later, but we still goin' out of town to take care that business."

In the streets, those that know what they are doing know that strategy is an art that they must master to survive. One must look beyond what's right in front of them; they must look beyond what's going on and calculate many steps ahead of the game. It requires focus and strict attention to the ultimate goal of survival. Others can get caught up in the hype, but those that are going to survive what comes their way are always on point. Ain't no love in the streets.

CHAPTER 2

Hours later, Chub and Trina were in a hotel room in Pennsylvania. Trina was knocked out in the bed sleeping like she'd worked over-time two days in a row. Chub on the other hand couldn't sleep at all. His mind was racing. Who couldn't figure out who would send somebody to kill him. He played fair in the game; at least he thought he did.

Sure he made a few moves here and there, but he never crossed anyone that didn't have it coming.

Looking out of the window, Chub watched a young black man exit a silver Camero. The young man was dressed in a black sweat suit with the hood pulled over his head. Chub was watching the man like a hawk until the man disappeared into a hotel room across the parking lot. He pulled out his phone and sent a text: Ay, slim, what's going on?

Moments later a text came back: It's on fire around here.

Chub was sure his man was talking about the murder. His man, Tony, lived in the building he was leaving when he ran into the dude with the baseball cap. Tony made his living dealing with fake money. Chub had been making moves with the fake money for a few months. He was making a killing working the fake money out of town. He was a bread winner for Tony.

The relationship between Tony and Chub was a good one to say the least, but at the present time Chub was looking at everyone like they were against him. After all, somebody had just tried to kill him.

Chub slid his phone back in his pocket and went in the bathroom. He turned on the water and began to wash his face with cold water. He was dead tiered, but he couldn't find it in him to go to sleep. Not even the bags under his eyes could force him to get some rest. His mind was set on making the move he had to make and then it was back to D.C. Looking in the mirror, Chub could see the effect stress was having on him. Late nights, grinding, and trips back and forth on the highway was getting to him.

Trina woke up when she heard the water running. She called out, "Chub, are you gonna' get some rest?"

"Yeah, baby. I just got a lot on my mind, you know how that goes. Shit way serious right now."

Ebony Chronicles of Elevation

"I understand that, but you gotta get some rest so you can be sharp when you go meet them peoples."

"Okay, T., I'm bout to come lay down in one second, cool?"

Trina didn't want to press Chub too much. She understood what he was going through and what he had on his mind. She'd been his woman for close to five years. Trina was 26 years old, two years younger than Chub. As far as the murder back in D.C., she wasn't really trippin' off what went down. She trusted Chub, she knew he could take care of the situation, plus whatever came with it.

Chub finished up washing his face and got in the bed with Trina. He wrapped his arms around her and said, "I really do need some rest."

"I know." Trina laid her head on his chest. "Just take your time, make this move and we goin' back home. You can get on top of everything. Get some rest now and clear your mind."

"You right." Chub kissed Trina on her lips and then put his arms behind his head and closed his eyes. He wasn't even going right to sleep; he was drifting into deeper thought. Nevertheless, minutes later he was sleep.

The sound of her cell phone grabbed Trina's attention. It was almost five in the morning. She rolled out of the bed, not waking Chub. Carefully she pulled her phone out of her Gucci bag. Looking over her shoulder to make sure Chub was still in a deep sleep. He was. She looked at the phone. There was a new text. The text made her nervous. It was from a guy by the name of Donnie. Donnie was a dude that owned a strip club in D.C. called Club Real Live. Trina used to dance at the club. She made a lot of money in the spot, in fact, she met Chub there.

Walking into the bathroom, Trina read the text: *You see what went down. Next time it won't go down like that.*

*Now get me my fuckin' money! This is the last time I'm gon'
say somethin' to you about this shit!*

The text made Trina nervous. She hated lying to
Chub. However, there was a part of her life that she kept
away from Chub. For a while, Trina transported cocaine for
Donnie. She would drive the drugs from the D.C. area to
other cities like Richmond, Philly, Newport, and Baltimore.
She was good at it and never had any fuck ups until her
very last trip. On her last trip she was car jacked in
Forestville, MD. More than $150, 000 worth of coke was
lost. Donnie blamed Trina for the lost and demanded that
she find a way to get him his money back as soon as
possible. At the time she only owed him $50,000, but
Donnie was pressing her hard. He even told her he would
have her and her man murdered. Trina had seen many
things in her young life. She had seen men smoked,
smoked in broad daylight. Donnie was one of those men
that she'd seen in action on the streets of D.C.

She couldn't sit in the bathroom and play the texting
game. She needed to speak to Donnie. She slid out of the
bathroom without making a sound. Chub was still in a
deep sleep. Carefully, Trina stepped out of the hotel room
and eased the door shut behind her. Her heart was racing.
She felt like her back was against the wall. Something had
to be done. She walked toward the steps as she hit
Donnie's name on her call log.

"You think I'm playing some type of games wit' you
about my paper, bitch?" Donnie answered the phone with a
deep, dark voice. The sound of his voice sent chills through
Trina's body.

She took a deep breath and whispered, "I'm gon' get
you the rest of—"

"You not movin' fast enough, bitch!"

Ebony Chronicles of Elevation

"Please, I told you I'm gon' get you your money. All I need is another few days. I got you a hundred-thousand in no time." Trina pleaded.

"Look here, bitch, get me the rest of my paper or you and that broke-ass nigga you fuckin' wit' gon' be a memory. Understand?"

"I understand, Donnie. I will have it."

"You better." Donnie hung up the phone.

Trina stood still holding the phone in here hand. Donnie's words shook her to her core. In her eyes, he was the wrong nigga to fuck with. She should have never dealt with him outside of working at his club. Once she crossed the line and made a few moves for Donnie he began to act like she was his woman. Things turned ugly when she shot down his attempts to get in her panties. Donnie could not believe that she wouldn't give him the pussy. None of the girls that worked at his clubs ever told him no when he cracked for the pussy. Trina was different, but she did jump at the chance to get some fast money when Donnie asked her if she'd move some work out of town for him.

"Trina! What you doin' out here?!"

Trina jumped. She turned around and saw Chub standing in the doorway of the hotel room. She felt like she'd been caught in the wrong. Quickly, she slid her phone back inside her bag and turned to face Chub with the guilty look on her face.

"Fuck is you out here on the phone wit'? Fuck is up wit' you?"

Trina was caught off guard; she didn't know how she wanted to play the situation. She didn't want to lie to Chub.

Chub headed down the steps and snatched her phone. "Fuck is up with you?" He began looking at the call log on her phone.

134

Trina had a nervous look on her face. "Chub, don't take it the wrong way."

With a frown on his face, Chub said, "Don't take it the wrong way? What way should I take it then, huh? You tell me! A nigga just tried to kill me and you sitting out here talking' to another nigga on the phone in secret. Fuck is up wit' you? The fuck is you playin' wit'? What the fuck you and Donnie got to talk about at this time of morning?"

"I can explain!" Trina shouted. "Let me explain!"

Chub gave Trina a serious look and said, "You better start explainin' then!"

"It's like this..." Trina came clean and told Chub the truth. She saw no other way to deal with the matter.

Chub didn't say a word although his anger and blood boiled. Nevertheless, he listened. He felt like Trina had crossed him, yet he still loved her. He wanted to understand what she was telling him. Rubbing his chin, Chub said, "How could you keep some shit like this from me? Fuck is wrong wit' you, Trina?"

"I didn't want to stress you, I wanted to take care of it myself but it got out of hand. I didn't know how to—"

"Fuck all that!" Chub snapped. "A nigga told you he would get me smoked and you ain't say shit to me. What the fuck is on your fuckin' mind?" he raised his voice.

Trina jumped. Chub had never put his hands on her before but at this very moment she felt like he was about to smack the shit out of her. "I didn't know what to do, Chub!"

"Fuck you mean, you didn't know what to do?" Chub let out a long sigh and shook his head. He was disgusted with Trina, at the moment he couldn't stand the sight of her. Turning his back to her, Chub headed for the hotel room.

Following close behind Chub, Trina called out, "Hold on, hold on, let me explain!"

Ebony Chronicles of Elevation

With anger in his eyes, Chub spent around and snapped, "Explain what?! Explain to me that a nigga tried to kill me tonight and you runnin' around here keepin' a bunch of secrets and shit?!"

"I didn't want you to get mad; I didn't want you to look at me in a different light. I love you. I love you with all my heart. You mean the world to me, Chub, you gotta believe me."

Chub gave her a long hard look. She had tears in her eyes. The sight moved Chub and curbed his anger enough to make him think about what she was talking about. Deep down inside he knew that she would never do anything to hurt him, at least that's what he wanted to believe.

"Trina, look here, you know how this shit go out here. You can't leave me in the dark with anything that goes on out on these streets. You gotta keep me on point at all times. No matter what."

"I know, I'm sorry, please believe me." Her voice was shaky and pleading. "Do you believe me?"

Chub said nothing for a second. All kinds of things were running through his mind. Trust was always a big issue with him in the life he lived. "Let's go inside."

Inside the hotel room Chub and Trina sat on the bed. Again, he asked her to explain everything to him. She did.

Rubbing his chin, Chub said, "I'm gon' have to deal wit' this nigga Donnie for real."

"No, all I have to do is give him his money and then I'm done with him. Nothing more, nothing less. You see what I'm sayin'?"

"I hear you, but the situation is bigger than that at this point. The nigga has threatened to kill us both. I have to deal wit' the situation in the right way. Simple as that."

Trina took a deep breath and said, "So how do you want to deal with it?"

"You already know." Chub said as his cell phone goes off. He pulled it out and looked at the screen. It was the man he was supposed to meet. He put a finger to his lips and told Trina to be quite. Answering the phone, he said, "What's good?"

"I'm ready for you. Be at the spot in thirty minutes." A voice said with a Spanish accent.

"I'll be there." Chub ended the call. Looking at Trina, he said, "I gotta make the move, stay right here until I get back. Don't be on the phone talkin' to nobody. Don't tell nobody where you are. You understand?"

"Yes, I understand. How long you gon' be gon'?"

"Not long, maybe an hour. I'll call you and let you know what's good, okay?"

Trina gave him a hug. "Be careful, baby."

"I will."

Street guys, like all other people, cannot survive if they don't know what is going on around them. They must always be looking out for what is coming next. If they are slick, they can paint a picture of weakness when they are strong so that they can be ready for whatever when it comes their way. Control the way things appear in the streets and know what's going on at all times.

Chapter 3

Chub let the Yo Gotti CD blast as he did 70 mph on the highway heading to meet the connect for the fake money. He was trying to focus on the move at hand, but at the same time he was thinking about what he would have to face as soon as he got back to D.C. His trust level was at an all time low. He didn't know who was really against him and wanted him to fall victim. No matter what, Chub refused to take a loss. Trina had him second-guessing her as well. He felt that out of all people, she was supposed to always make the right move when it came to him and her. At the time, he wasn't going to sweat the situation too much. He loved Trina and nothing could change that.

Donnie was a more serious situation. Chub knew that he was going to have to be on his A-game to deal with Donnie in any kind of way. Nevertheless, Donnie could get it as far as Chub was concerned. The only question was; 'what was the best way to get at Donnie and get away with it.' Chub knew his money wasn't long enough to deal with Donnie head up; he had to do it in a way that Donnie wouldn't see it coming. Easier said than done, but anything was possible when Chub put his mind to it.

Stress was coming from all directions. Chub lit an Al Capone cigar as he pulled up in the shopping mall right off of the highway. He parked and looked around to see if anything was out of place. That was always a habit of his. He took a long hard pull on the cigar as he cut the car off. Pulling out his cell phone he called his man Tony.

"What's good, slim?" Tony answered the phone.

"I'm at the spot, I'm 'bout to go take care of this shit. I'll be back in the city before the night. Cool?"

"Yeah, that's a bet, slim." Tony said.

Something in Tony's voice didn't sit well with Chub, it sounded like something was wrong.

Chub said, "Is everything cool on your end, homie?"

Tony sighed. "I'm good, I'll holla at you when you get back in the city. Focus on what you doing, we'll talk."

Chub didn't like that. He needed to know what was going on. He said, "Ay, my man, you need to put me on point if something ain't right. I got too much shit on my mind to be worrying about some shit that's going on, so just spit it out."

"Not over the phone, Chub. Handle your business, okay?"

Chub sighed. "Okay, cool." He ended the call and got out of the car. Looking around the parking lot he laid eyes on the car repair spot that was the meeting location. Popping the trunk he grabbed a gym bag containing $25,000. With a firm grip on the bag he headed for the car repair joint.

Walking through the door of Easton Auto, Chub asked for Alex. A pretty Spanish girl got up and walked into the back. Chub had to take a look at that ass as she stepped. Moments later she returned and told Chub to head to the back to see Alex.

Once he entered the back, Chub saw three well dressed Spanish men shooting pool. Sports Center was on the huge flat screen TV. The tallest of the three turned to face Chub and said, "My friend, it's always good to see you." He extended his hand.

Chub shook his hand. "It's always good to see you as well, Alex."

Alex smiled and nodded. "Follow me Chub."

Chub followed Alex through another door into a plush office. The office was laid out. Fish tank with sharks. Two huge flat screens—Soccer was on one TV and basketball on the other. Alex lit a Cuban cigar and blew smoke in the air. He was a man with confidence.

Chub had too much on his mind to sit around and kick it with Alex. He sat the gym bag on the desk and said, "All the bread is here, Alex. I'm kinda in a rush, got a few pressin' things goin' on back home. No disrespect."

Shaking his head in agreement; Alex said, "No disrespect taken, Chub. I understand how things go out here in the real world." Alex took a look at the money in

Ebony Chronicles of Elevation

the gym bag. "I have all fifties for you this time. It's the best money you are going to see on the East Coast, it spends anywhere."

"Okay. That's what I need to hear right now." Chub said. His mind was on his conversation with Tony. He wondered what the fuck was going on that Tony couldn't talk about.

Alex said, "I'll be right back, Chub." He left the room and returned with a mid-size duffle bag. He dropped it on the floor and unzipped it. Stack of fifty dollar bills were all that could be seen. "It's one-hundred-thousand. You can count it if you like."

Shaking his head against counting the fake money, Chub said, "I take your word. I really gotta get back on the road."

"I understand, Chub." Alex walked closer to Chub, close enough to whisper. He blew smoke in the air and said in a low voice, "I would love for you to work for me, Chub. Just think about it. You are trustworthy and I respect that in a man. There's lot of money to be made out here for the right kind of guy with his mind focused and his heart in the right place. You understand where I'm coming from?"

Chub nodded. "I understand, but I have too much on my plate right now. I might have to take you up on that at another time, if possible."

With a pat on Chub's shoulder, Alex said, "I understand. Call me when you think you want to take me up on that."

"Will do." Chub shook Alex's hand and left with the duffle bag.

Outside, Chub walked across the parking lot carefully. Once at the car he popped the trunk and threw the duffle bag inside. Shutting the trunk, Chub took a deep breath. Rubbing his chin, he shook his head as he thought about what he would have to face once he got back to D.C. He jumped in the car and headed back to the hotel.

Everybody has limitations, no matter how hard they go. They can have countless soldiers on their team. That can only take them so far in the streets when things get out of hand. One must know his limits and pick his battles wisely. Consider the unseen, plan for the worse, and give all of your effort to the cause of victory.

Chapter 4

Chub walked into the hotel room and saw Trina laying on the bed looking at TV. He wasted no time saying, "Let's go. I want to hit the road now. I got shit to do when we get back to the city."

"Okay." Trina said, gathering her things.

They jumped in the car and hit the highway without a lot of talking. Chub was in deep thought and Trina could tell. Trina wanted to know where Chub's mind was but knew he would open up in a few. Her mind drifted to the situation with Donnie. She hoped it wouldn't hurt her relationship with Chub. He was the love of her life. She wanted to put the whole thing behind her.

Chub cut his eyes at Trina and said, "Call the nigga, Donnie."

With a confused look on her face, Trina said, "Huh?"

"You heard me, call the nigga, Donnie. I need to holla at him."

"I don't think that's a good idea, baby." Trina didn't want the situation to get any worse than it already was.

"Trina!" Chub snapped. "Call the nigga before I do. Don't question me on this one."

Ebony Chronicles of Elevation

"Ok." Trina said, reluctantly. She pulled out her cell phone and called Donnie. Handing Chub the phone she sighed and said, "What are you going to say?"

"Watch and see. I want to go ahead and put it all on the table with this nigga." Chub said as the phone rang.

"What's up, Trina? You got my money?" Donnie said. There was music playing in the background.

"This ain't Trina, this her man, Chub. You know me."

Donnie snickered. "Yeah, I'm hip to you. Why are you calling me? You got some bread for me? I don't want no shorts. Your woman owes me, if you ain't got the money it ain't no reason for us to even be on the phone rappin."

"Ay look, I ain't call you for us to be talking all slick and shit. I called you to handle some business, if you can't talk business then we can end the call and get into whatever comes next. I'm just trying to settle all scores if I can, so me and my woman can move on without looking over our shoulders. Simple as that. Do you want the paper she owes you or not?"

Donnie was silent for a second. He thought about what Chub was saying. He wanted to carry Chub and say fuck him. Deep inside, he didn't give a fuck about the money. Secretly he wanted Trina and was fucked up that he couldn't have her. He didn't understand how a nigga like Chub could have such a hold on the heart of a woman like Trina. After all, in Donnie's mind, Chub didn't have enough money to ever keep a woman that Donnie wanted.

"You still there?" Chub asked.

"Yeah, I want the paper. When you gon' bring it?"

"Tonight. How bout that? I give you the paper and that's the end of it."

"Cool. Call me when you ready." Donnie ended the call.

Chub handed the phone back to Trina and said, "I'm surprised at you, for real-for real."

"Chub, don't be like that, baby. I told you I didn't know what to do. I would never do anything to hurt you or make you not trust me. You know I love you with all my heart."

Chub kept a firm grip on the wheel with a dead stare ahead as he flew along the highway in a rush to get back to D.C. His mind was made up. He knew exactly how he wanted to deal with everything when he got back home. In a low and claim voice, Chub said, "You fucked up, Trina. You know how this shit goes out here. Trina, when a nigga talking about hurting you or me you come right to me about it, no matter what. You know this."

"I know, baby. I just didn't know what to do. It'll never happen again. I promise."

"It don't even matter." Chub said in a cold voice.

"What does that mean, what are you talking about?" Trina asked carefully.

"Imma smoke Donnie. It ain't no way around it." Chub said, never taking an eye off the road. "It ain't no other way to address this. A nigga ain't gon' rock me to sleep and take me out when I ain't paying attention." He cut his eyes at Trina. "We gon' go back home, I'ma take care of this shit and then we gon' hit the road and lay low for a while. You got it?"

Trina nodded her head. "Okay."

***

A few hours later Chub and Trina were back home in D.C. Inside their bedroom Chub was changing clothes. He was wasting no time getting down to business. His first stop was going to see Tony and then he would deal with Donnie.

Ebony Chronicles of Elevation

Trina sat on the bed wondering how things were going to turn out for the night. She didn't want Chub to get himself killed or locked up but she knew that there was nothing she could do to stop him once he had his mind made up. Nevertheless, something inside of her told her that things were about to ugly.

Trina had to speak her mind. She took a deep breath and said, "Chub, I really want you to let me deal with this Donnie situation. I don't want you to get in no trouble."

In a very calm voice, Chub said, "You should've thought about that before you decided to keep a secret from me. Shit is too close to home now. Do I need to remind you that somebody tried to kill me last night. I need to be askin' you if you have somethin' to hide from me."

"You talkin' crazy now, Chub. I don't have anything to hide from you ever. You know that. Don't act like that with me, baby."

Tucking a pistol into his waistband, Chub said, "Well, just sit back and let me do what I see fit." He kissed her on the forehead and left the room.

Trina sat there for a second and shook her head. She was trying her best to come up with a game plan in her mind to correct what was already set in motion. Her heart raced. Seconds later she heard the front door open and close. Getting up slowly she walked to the window and looked outside. She saw Chub get into the car and pull off. Shaking her head, Trina grabbed her cell phone. Going straight to her call log she selected the contact and made the call.

***

Pistol in his waistband and a duffle bag full of fake money in his hand, Chub knocked on Tony's door. For

144

years, Tony was always a dude Chub felt that he could trust somewhat. However, with all that was going on in his life at the time Chub didn't know who he could trust.

Tony answered the door wearing a white T-shirt, a pair of gym shorts, and a pair of slippers. He was a big man, could have been a football player if life would have taken him in that direction.

Chub stepped inside and dropped the duffle bag on the living room floor. He got straight to the point. "What were you talking about earlier?"

Tony lit a Newport and gave Chub a serious stare. News traveled fast in his line of work. "You know the nigga Donnie, right?"

"Yeah. Why?" Chub said, wondering why Donnie's name was coming up again.

"That's who tried to get you smoked. Word came to me not too long ago. I just didn't want to have the conversation over the phone. You know how that goes, right?"

"No doubt, I understand. Ain't no thing. I'm gon' have a talk wit' Donnie tonight as a matter of fact. He fuckin' wit' the right one this go 'round."

Tony nodded as he bent over to unzip the duffle bag. "You got your break-down already, right?"

Chub nodded.

"Ay, look here though, Chub. Don't play wit' this nigga Donnie. He been around for a while, doing dirt and all, you don't last as long as he has lasted if you don't know what you are doin'. He's on his toes and his paper's right. Keep that in mind, no matter what you do, feel me?"

"Yeah, I know. So let me ask you this: How did you get word that Donnie was behind the hit on me?"

Tony raised his eyebrows and said, "Because it happened to close to my spot for me not to know what was

Ebony Chronicles of Elevation

going on. I checked a few traps and got the info I was looking for. You know how this shit goes."

"I feel you." Chub said, feeling the pressure of what was at hand.

"One more thing, Chub ..."

"What's that?"

"Trina, man ..."

"What about Trina?" Chub said with a serious tone.

"Trina ain't right, Chub."

"What you mean she ain't right?" Chub wasn't feeling Tony saying anything about Trina. She was his heart, his everything. She could do no wrong in his eyes.

"Trina fucks wit' that nigga Donnie. Now I don't know if she was working the nigga or what, but she's closer to him than you think. I'm just putting you on point. Don't be fucked up at me. I'm just giving you what I got when I checked into the nigga Donnie and what he got going on out here on these streets."

Chub was speechless for a second. He refused to believe that Trina would really cross him. Before he could say anything his cell phone sounded off with Trina's ringtone. He pulled the phone out of his pocket and answered it. "What's up, Trina?" "It ain't Trina, nigga. If you to see her alive again you will get your ass in your car and get back home as fast as you can." The person on the other end, ended the call.

Chub felt his heart drop. His palms got sweaty and he began to get warm.

Tony could tell that there was something very wrong. "You okay.""I gotta go, Tony. I'll call you later." Chub left the apartment in a hurry. His heart rate was at an all time high as he ran down the steps to the back door. He bolted out of the door and up the step to the alley and jumped in his car. His thoughts were all over the place, but the only thing that mattered was making sure that Trina was okay.

146

Not knowing what he was going to be facing when he got to his house had Chub gripping his pistol, ready for whatever.

As he drove down his street he didn't see anything out of place on the block. He drove by his house slowly; still nothing looked out of place. Chub drove around the block. Still, he saw nothing out of place. Finally he decided to pull up behind the house by driving through the alley. He parked the car and got out, pistol in hand. Looking around as if a death trap was waiting for him around every corner, Chub made his way to the back door of the house; it was slightly open. He looked at the locks and could tell that it had been kicked open. Cocking the hammer on his pistol, Chub slowly entered the back door. Raising his pistol, ready to shoot, he entered the kitchen. All was clear. Stepping into the living room Chub couldn't believe his eyes: Trina was tied to a chair with a strip of duck tape over her mouth. She'd been slapped around a few times according to the looks of her battered face. A masked gunman was standing behind her with a shotgun to the back of her head. Another masked gunman was sitting on Chub's sofa with a MAC-11 in his hand.

The gunman on the sofa aimed his weapon at Chub and said in a calm voice, "Don't even think about no gangsta shit or you and your bitch gon' die in this muthafucka', believe that. So go ahead and drop your heat."

Chub's eyes darted back and forth between the gunman and Trina. Trina had tears in her eyes. She was struggling to say something but the duck tape wouldn't let her get her words out.

"Don't make me ask you again, homeboy." the gunman on the sofa said with a murderous seriousness.

The gunman with the shotgun smacked Trina in the back of the head with the butt of weapon. She yelled with

Ebony Chronicles of Elevation

all of the sound coming through her nose. "Put the joint down, nigga!" the gunman yelled.

Trina was jumping up and down in her seat, shaking her head, trying her best to tell Chub something.

The gunman on the sofa stood up and said, "Chub, do you want to die right here, or do you want to hear what I have to say?"

Chub was between a rock and hard place. He could've went hard and let the gunplay begin, but felt that Trina would be dead for sure if things went down that way. As he began to lower his weapon a thought crossed his mind about death. He felt that if he gave up his heat that he would be dead man anyway. He went for the home run and fired his weapon at the gunman with the shotgun. The first three shots went off hitting the gunman in the chest, knocking him against the wall. The gunman with the MAC-11 fired, hitting Chub in the neck and arm. Chub fell to the ground and began to fire at the gunman with the MAC-11, hitting him a few times somewhere in the upper body. The shotgun went off two times back to back; buck shots sprayed the wall above Chub's head.

Trina was going crazy, tied to the chair. She managed to knock herself to the floor as the gunshots went off.

Chub took aim at the gunman with the shotgun and hit him right between the eyes with a perfect shot. Killing him.

The gunman with the MAC-11 charged at Chub, hitting Chub in the stomach a few more times before bolting out of the backdoor.

Fading in and out of reality, Chub crawled over to Trina, with blood everywhere. He struggled to untie her.

Once Trina was loose all she could scream was, "Oh my God, I'm so sorry, I'm so sorry! This is all my fault!"

She grabbed Chub and held him tight, getting blood all over.

"You need to get out of here; I'm not going to make it. I'm hit too bad." Chub said, struggling to breathe.

"I'm so sorry. I should have listened to you, this is all my fault."

In almost a whisper, Chub said, "What's your fault?"

"I called Donnie, I called him and tried to deal with this myself. I didn't want you to get hurt or killed. I should have listened to you. I swear I didn't mean for this to happen."

Chub couldn't believe his ears. He couldn't believe Trina was the cause of so much drama. "How ... how could you?"

"I didn't think—"

Before Trina could get another word out, the gunman with the MAC-11 reappeared through the back door spraying his weapon. Shots hit Trina in the head; killing her instantly. The gunman then stood over Chub and said, "Pussy, a nigga's quickest down fall." He then hit Chub in the head five times with the MAC-11.

Slowly, the gunman looked around and walked out of the house.

Donnie will be pleased that Chub and Trina are dead and gone.

Street life is so real; it affects some people in more ways than one. I myself have lost so many people close to me because of the street life. The stories I write are not to glorify the game, but to paint a realistic picture of what goes on in the underworld. This story is dedicated to my man Richard "Black" Bracey. Things that he went through and the loved ones he lost to a situation like this will forever weigh heavy on my heart and live in my mind.
Real is back!

My Heart

Chris Hicks

"Who is it?" asked Tavon as he walked over to the front door, "It's me Amber, stop playing boy." With a grin on his face and butterflies in his stomach, Tavon answered the door.

"What's up baby girl" he said, followed by a passionate kiss on her lips as she walked in. This was her first visit to Tavon's new spot, after moving out of his Dad's place for the second and he hoped the last time. Work had been slow in the construction industry for the past two years, causing him to bite his pride and go back under his father's roof.

Application after application, interview after interview, and finally, one of the job opportunities came through, he just hoped this time it would hold up

"Have a seat," he said as he motioned her to the leather couch that he just removed from storage. Amber was beaming with excitement about his new two bedroom apartment, mainly because it was only fifteen minutes from her house and could make as much noise as she wanted while making love. His dad was cool, but not that cool.

She began taking off her black pumps and rested her pedicure toes on the carpet as they talked. With a comfortable and relaxed look she asked "Where is Destiny?"

Tavon screamed out "Destiny! Amber is here." Immediately this cute, brown skin, five year-old with long silky hair ran out of her room and gave Amber a big hug. As if on cue, Tavon's ringtone of dogs barking went off.

Upon hearing this, his face and whole disposition changed dramatically like he just got laid off for the sixth time. The phone continued ringing as Tavon picked it up, but not answer. Destiny, while still in Amber's arms, cries out "Daddy why you not answering your phone?" Taking in a deep breath, Tavon finally answers.

"It's about got damn time you no good piece of shit" the sassiest, rudest voice you ever heard before in your life screeched through the line. It was Tina, Destiny's mother."What bitch you got around my daughter?" she yelled. Destiny and Amber starred up at Tavon as he got up and went into the kitchen for some privacy.

Tina and Tavon were not strangers to having disagreements with each other, in fact, their last argument was only two days ago. Tina had decided, in the middle of the school year to take Destiny on a two week long vacation to New York to see one of her many boyfriends, without telling him. Not knowing the whereabouts of his daughter, Tavon blew up her phone without once getting a response.

Together they were known as "TNT" to everyone because they always blew up at each other. Tina had an erratic temper, basically she was a ticking time bomb, liable to go off at any second for any reason. She hated the fact that Destiny was a Daddy's girl, always wanting to be around her father.

Tina still held resentment towards him, because Tavon broke up with her after he heard, then saw a sex tape that she made with one of his boys. Hate and jealousy always stood in the way with Tina towards Tavon so it was hard for her to move on with her life as he clearly has done. It was clear as day in her head that the both of them were still together and only temporarily separated.

Tavon, with a look of disgust on his face, sat down in the kitchen with the phone to his ear. Listening to her talking about who Tavon's company was," I thought I told

Ebony Chronicles of Elevation

you not to have none of your bitches around my daughter". Tavon pulls the phone from his ear, looks at it and thinks to himself, "I can't believe this shit, here we go again."

Tina, who was home at the time doing her regular check up on Tavon whenever he had Destiny, didn't want any other women around her child but her and she always made that clear. Tavon didn't believe in having random women around Destiny, just wasn't his style. Actually during the last four months, Amber was the only women he was seeing. Though Tina, with her insecurities, always thought Tavon had different women around Destiny, even when they were together. Tina continued ranting and raving about how Destiny doesn't need to be around any other women except her, while Tavon continued to listen in disgust. He had had enough and was about to hang up when she blurted out, "I'm coming to get my damn daughter."

"No you not, that's not what we agreed and besides you just had her for two weeks." Without responding, Tina hung up the. Amber, still sitting on the couch with Destiny, could tell Tavon was upset and asked was everything ok, he replied "no, you know who is on her way to come get Destiny".

As Tavon returned back to the living room to sit on the couch to try to relax before Tina arrived, he thought to his self that this was going to be the first time that Amber and Tina would meet.

Unlike Tina, Amber was the quiet type, very soft spoken, and believed in being a lady and a professional first, though she will get down if she had to. All the stories she heard about Tina and her character, Amber felt like she already knew her. As Destiny went back to her room, Amber and Tavon waited, within 15 minutes, Tina was knocking at the door.. As he answered door, Tina screamed, "Where is Destiny? I'm not playing, where is my child?"

152

"Calm down woman." Tavon expressed. "You not taking her and that's that, don't make me call the police on you. I'm not playing with you".

Unbeknownst to them both, Amber was calling the authorities." Man, fuck the police, call them, I don't give a fuck", Tina sad pushing her way in. Going into the living room and upon seeing Amber on the phone, she screamed out."Who the fuck is this bitch" Amber stood up and said "who you calling bitch, bitch?"

As Tina began to move toward Amber, Tavon ran in between to separate them as Amber, with the phone still in her hand, yelled "hurry up" and hung up the phone."This is my man house, and that's our daughter, you need to leave" Tina said. Destiny, who was in her room at the time, could hear all of the fussing and upon recognizing her mother's voice, came running in. Tina looked towards Destiny but continued to argue with Amber and Tavon. "Go back in your room" Tavon said, but Destiny, with tears in her eyes, just stood there scared.

While all that commotion was going on inside, outside two police cars with their lights flashing pulled up to the apartment complex, three of the four officers proceeded to approach the door. A minute or so later a third police car arrives.. As soon as the officers came on the complex, they could hear all the commotion. Running towards the noise, they knocked on the door to Tevon's apartment, announcing, "Police, open the door!" Tavon ran over to the door, as he noticed the flashing lights though the dining room window. The three officers cautiously walked in the apartment; Amber walked over to one of the officers and told him that she was the one who made the call. While explaining what happened, Tina proceeded to talk to one of the other officers and told him that she just came to pick up her daughter. Tavon just stood there with his head down and his hands over his face, not believing

Ebony Chronicles of Elevation

what was happening. Thinking, "I just moved into this place, suppose to start this gig tomorrow. I thought things were finally starting to turn around"". Just as he started to think to himself what else could go wrong, that's when Tina yelled out, "He hit me".

Tavon, with disbelief, lifted his head up after hearing Tina's lie and Amber, shocked, stopped her conversation. "NO, NO, NO", Tavon shouted shaking his head as Tina broke down in tears saying "He choked me, hit me and pushed me, and she stood there and watched". Amber and Tavon both started to explain to the three officers that Tina was lying, but that only made her cry harder. "Where's my baby" she cried out. One of the officers told Tina to go and get Destiny. Tavon and Amber continued to convince the officers that Tina was lying as she went to retrieve Destiny. "What's wrong mommy?" she asked, "nothing baby, daddy was being bad and he has to go bye-bye" Once Tina and Destiny came back to the main room, one of the officers asked Tavon to follow him down stairs. "For what I didn't do anything?" Tavon demanded. Amber started to tear up because she knew what was going to happen next. Tina, with Destiny in her arms walked past the officers, Tavon and Amber, yelling out "and I'm pressing charges" and proceeded to her car.

There were three other officers standing outside talking, when Tina stepped out the door of the apartment complex. One of the officers said, "What's up Tina, how you been girl" with a grin on his face thinking about that last blow job she gave. She looked up and said "O, hey Rodney", then proceeded to her car and start her car. As Tina waited impatiently to see if they were going to lock Tavon up for the lies she just told, Rodney came over. "What happen and don't lie neither?" he said. Tina began to tell him her made up side of the story, while Rodney just stood there listening.

He had an expression on his like he had heard this type of story a thousand times.

The police officers brought Tavon out of the apartment complex in handcuffs and, proceeded to put him in the back of the police car. One of the officers who was talking to Tina inside the apartment, came over to her car and begin to explain what was going to happen to Tavon next and what she needed to do.

Amber stayed inside of the apartment crying; she was very upset and emotional, she stared out the window until the police and Tina left. She then called Mr. Lester, who was Tavon's father, and told him what happened. Mr. Lester was furious, but tried to calm Amber down by telling her that everything was going to be ok.

Morning came after Tavon's first arrest and Amber and Mr. Lester went down to central booking to see what the charge was. His charge was 3rd degree assault, but he couldn't be released until he saw the commissioner, and she didn't know how long that was going to take. At this point, Amber was in complete shock as the officer spoke, but Tavon's father appeared cool and decided to wait in the lobby.

What was supposed to be an in and out visit became an all day marathon. By the time Tavon was released. the day was over with. It was now six o'clock in the evening. When Tavon first walked out Amber immediately stood up and ran to him with emotions on her face and arms opened wide.. With tears of joy she said, "Are you ok, I missed you" Tavon replied "It was only one night, not a year" with a grin on his face as he proceeded to give Amber a long kiss. "Damn boy, your breath stink" Amber said smiling like she just hit the lottery. Mr. Lester, relieved but impatient, stood up and yelled "Come on you two, I'm tired, shit".

They drove Tavon back to his apartment. He was so mad and frustrated, not because he was just arrested, but

Ebony Chronicles of Elevation

because he missed his first day at the job. When he made it home, immediately went over to his phone, picked it up and started to check his messages. Out of the fives voice messages, three of them was his new job, two asking where he was and the third, explaining t they were going to find someone else to replace him. Tavon's face showed his sadness and he yelled out "shit", his father and girlfriend looked at him and didn't need to ask what happened."I just can't catch a break" he said as his stomach turned."Every time things start to turn around for me something always goes wrong." Amber tried to console him. "Baby don't worry, another job will come thru for you", as she walked over to him and begin to hug him. "It's going to be fine" she said. Tavon didn't respond he just fell into her warm embrace as his father began to dose off. He was so tired from being at the central bookings all day, but then rose up off the couch and told his heart broken son to call him if he needed anything then walked out the door to go home.

After this long day, they just wanted to rest and Tavon just wanted to wake from this nightmare. It was now close to ten o'clock and Tavon's phone began to ring, of course it was the barking ringtone again. "I'm not getting it, last time I picked it up, I ended up in jail." he said while looking at Amber. He got up and turned the phone off and climbed back in bed with Trying to lighten the mood, Amber said, "Hey, your favorite show' on, Cops", they both started to laugh out. It had been a long day for them both as they dosed off to sleep.

The next morning, Tavon sat up in bed and turned on his phone and checked his voice messages, one was from Missy, Tina's cousin. She stated that he needed to come get Destiny from her house. Without hesitation, Tavon immediately jumped out of the bed and threw on some clothes. He knew something was wrong but he didn't know exactly what, but needed to get to Destiny. His minded drifted to Tina and then to Destiny, his heart. Amber who was still in the bed asked him what was wrong but Tavon just said to her "Call me on your lunch break and I will know by then". Amber with a confused look on her face simply replied "ok" and then Tavon dashed out the apartment.

When Tavon arrived at Missy's house, Destiny greeted him at the door, saying "hey daddy" as picked her and gave her the biggest hug.

Missy walked into the living room and before she could speak, Tavon asked her what was wrong. "Not in front of the tv" she said, talking to Tavon in code. Tavon then asked Destiny to go upstairs into Missy's room. Once Destiny left to go upstairs, Missy began to explain what happened and why Destiny was with her instead of Tina. She started off by saying that Tina got pulled over in New York for speeding and because she was so nervous, the police checked her car and found drugs. They locked her up for drug possession. "How could that bitch put my daughter in a situation like that?" he mumbled to himself

Missy continue to explain that Tina must have known that they were going to lock her up because she called her and told her to come get Destiny, she didn't want the state to take her. But it was kind of too late. The officers must have called somebody at the child protective services, but they did let Missy bring Destiny home to her father. Tavon begin to feel even more stressed out, with the lost of his new job, being in jail all night and now this situation. "What's next?" he pondered.

Missy then pulled out some documents and gave them to him. Tavon began to look over the documents. "It says somebody is coming to my house today" Tavon said, Missy then said "let me see that" she then grabbed the document and begins to look them over. "Have you heard from Tina yet" he asked, "No" Missy replied. "How much

Ebony Chronicles of Elevation

drugs did she have in the car?" Tavon questioned with disgust on his face. "I don't know" Missy replied. Tavon knew she was lying, but didn't have time to argue with her, he had to get back to his apartment before the social worker did. He couldn't lose Destiny too.

Once Tavon and Destiny left Missy's house they began to travel home. He began to reflect back on his life and the last 24hrs. Looking over at Destiny, who is the only reason for being on this earth and his "heart", was the main reason why he was stressed out. Tavon always felt that it was his responsibility to provide for Destiny, it was his responsibility to make sure she didn't want for nothing. Determined that he wasn't going to be one of those fathers who were never around to take care of their kids, he was going to be better than that. He had a model. He saw that his father was there for him, even now, and took care of the family. He wanted to do the same for his. It was a stressful time because his plans, which was to get better and be in a better position so he could take care of Destiny, seem like they were falling apart in front of his very eyes.

Arriving at the apartment, Destiny immediately went back to her room and turned on the TV to her favorite station, the Disney Network.

Tavon started to clean up to prepare for the social worker. After about 20min of cleaning, he sat on his couch and his phone began to ring again, this time it was Amber. She, being concerned, immediately started to ask Tavon what happened but as he started to explain the story that Missy told him there was a knock at the door. Tavon told her that he had to call her back because the social worker was at the door. This made Amber even more confused and doubly worried for both him and Destiny. She knew more than anything that Destiny was his heart and started to hope for the best. Tavon walked over to the door and asked who it was. A lady with a soft voice said "Ms. Hopkins". He opened the door and invited her in the apartment and motioned her to have a seat.

After the last 24 hours plus, he was feeling a little nervous because he didn't know what to expect, but he had always heard stories about how strict the state was with parents and the well being of their kids. Ms. Hopkins was a African American women in her mid thirty's, medium built and wearing a dress suit. She had a look on her face like she was very concerned. "Do you know why I am here" she asked. Tavon replied "I think so." Ms. Hopkins then begin to explain that she was sent by the state because Tina was arrested on drug possession with Destiny in her custody, she also explained that he was now going to get 'temporary' full custody until a court date is issued. Next she asked about his relationship with Tina and her behavior. He then reluctantly began to tell Ms Hopkins about Tina's crazy and erratic behavior. Ms. Hopkins had a expression on her face like she was watching her favorite soaps all while writing in her notebook. Once he finished, he then asked to see Destiny. Tavon told her that she was sleep but sleep or not, he went. She was out cold, and then his phone began to ring with the dogs barking ringtone again. Destiny finally woke up and he asked her to come in the living room to meet someone special. Both of them walked backed into the living room where Ms. Hopkins was. "Your phone was ringing." Ms. Hopkins said to Tavon as he sat on the couch. Destiny then sat down next to him. "Well, here she is, this is Destiny, my heart" Tavon said to Ms. Hopkins. Destiny with her head resting against her father's arm and half asleep, said "hello" to Ms. Hopkins. "How are you today Destiny, you're a cute girl" she said with a smile on her face. Destiny looked up and smiled backed.

Tavon's phone began to ring again, it was the same ringtone, but he couldn't ignore it because he knew Tina was going to keep calling until he answered it. Tavon then

Ebony Chronicles of Elevation

said "excuse me Ms. Hopkins, I have to take this call" with the same look on his face like when he found out that he lost his job yesterday. Ms. Hopkins gave him a look like she knew who it was and said "no problem, this princess can keep me company" Tavon got up and grabbed his phone, and walked into his room. Ms. Hopkins then began to make small talk with Destiny.

Tavon answered his phone and said "What happened?" Tina who was home at this time didn't answer, instead she said "where is my baby, and why is she with you, Missy is suppose to be watching her not you" at this point Tavon was frustrated because he realized that Tina was trying to cover up her arrest. "Are you going to answer my question or not Tina" she said "what question" Tavon replied." What happened to you last night after you got me locked up?" Tina said "Nothing, I'm coming to get Destiny and if you try to stop me I'm going to call the police on you again" then Tina hung up the phone. He just sat on the bed and thought to himself how stupid can one person be. It was clear that Tina didn't know that Tavon had full custody of Destiny and it was even clearer that Tina didn't know that the social worker was at the apartment. Tina had caused so much drama to Tavon in the last 24hrs that it could have broken him mentally.

This time it was clear to Tavon that he had the upper hand now and it was time to settle all of the confusion once and for all. He knew he didn't have much time before Tina arrived so he had to think quick. He then went into the living room with Destiny and Ms. Hopkins who were laughing at each other. He then asked Destiny to go to her room for a few minutes. Ms. Hopkins looked at Tavon and knew something was going on, and then Tavon started to explain that Tina was on her way to come get Destiny. The more Ms. Hopkins listened, the more she begin to get upset, she then told Tavon not to worry about a thing and Tina's

160

not taking Destiny. Tavon, for a second felt at ease but knew Tina wasn't going to leave without a fight. Ms. Hopkins then told him not to feed into any of her lies and drama and just let her talk to her when she arrives. Ms. Hopkins was a great counselor; she calmed Tavon down and told him to relax.

Within 15 minutes Tavon phone began to ring, it was Tina, Ms. Hopkins looked up at Tavon and said "you ready," Tavon replied "O yeah" he then answered his phone "where my baby at?" Tina said in her sassy voice. Tavon didn't even bother to answer the question, instead he said, "you know you can't take her, and if you wouldn't have hung up the phone on me earlier you would have known that " Tina then said "what are you talking about, I'm outside ,bring Destiny down here...now" Tavon looked at Ms. Hopkins in disgust and said "she just doesn't get it!" Tina heard what Tavon said and got upset," who the fuck you talking to" she said while hanging up the phone and sashaying her way to his apartment. Tavon then looked at Ms. Hopkins and said "she's coming up," Ms. Hopkins said. That's fine," within a couple of minutes Tina started to bang on the door. Tavon opened the door and Tina stormed in."Where the fuck is my child" she said, Ms. Hopkins stood up and said "excuse me, watch your mouth!" Tina began to walk over to Ms. Hopkins and said "and who the fuck are you and why are you even here?" Tavon rushed in between the both of them and said "Tina you are way out of line" then Tina said "no, this bitch is out of line" Tina then tried to push him out of the way as if she was trying to get to Ms. Hopkins, then Tavon said "I'm bout to call the police on you." Tina yelled "call em, you know what happened the last time? Call the police bitch"

Destiny, who was still in her room, heard all the noise and ran out to see what was going on, she cried out "what wrong daddy?" Tavon immediately ran over to her and picked her up, and walked back into her room. He told

Ebony Chronicles of Elevation

Destiny that her mother was upset and to stay in the room. Kissed her on the forehead and told her "I love you". Destiny then grabbed one of his legs and started to hug it, saying "don't leave me daddy, I'm scared", "Destiny please let go of my leg, I'm coming right back, I promise" Tavon said. Destiny finally loosened up on Tavon's leg and jumped back on the bed, and then she picked up her brush and started to comb her dolls hair.

When Tavon went back into the living room, Tina was in Ms. Hopkins face with her finger pointed at it. Ms. Hopkins could see the anger and hurt in Tina's eyes and it tickled her a little that she thinks they are dating. When Tavon walked back in the living room, Tina's rage began to get worse, like the sight of his face triggered it. Tina backed out of Ms. Hopkins face and turned her anger to Tavon and said "I told you I didn't want none of your bitches around my daughter, you don't fucking listen." In an angry voice Tavon said "it's not even like that" but Tina was at the point where she didn't want to hear what he had to say. While Tina was in Tavon's face Ms. Hopkins noticed lights flashing on the dining room wall, she walked over to the dining room window and looked outside and saw two police cars. She felt a bit of relief for the moment because she didn't know what she was going to do with Tina. She then walked back into the living room. Now Tina had her hand on Tavon's face, then she pushed Tavon out of the way, and ran past Ms. Hopkins into the kitchen. Her hands were shaking because she was angry and nervous; she had two dark black mascara lines coming down her cheeks from crying. She pulled out a sharp knife from the kitchen and walked back out and stood in the doorway with the knife hidden in her hand. Tavon nor Ms. Hopkins could see it and she had every intention on hurting whoever stood in her way of taking Destiny home.

162

Destiny who was still in her room wanted to see what was going on and saw Tina in the kitchen doorway and ran out to her. Tavon saw Destiny running towards Tina and said "Go back in your room!" but she didn't listen and ran right to her mother. While Ms. Hopkins was going into the living room there was a knock on the door, it was the police.

Ms. Hopkins didn't even bother to ask who it was she just opened the door and the officers walked in and said that somebody in the building called about a loud commotion. When Tina saw it was the police she broke down again, and said "All I want is my baby and they won't let me take her, I have custody of her" The officer told Tina to calm down, then Tina said with tears running down her face," He hit me again" Ms. Hopkins couldn't believe what she was hearing and pulled out her state ID and showed it to the officer," I'm with the state. Sir as you can see I'm a social worker working on this case" she continued to tell the officer that Tavon was granted full custody of Destiny not Tina. Then Ms. Hopkins showed the officer her papers. Tina was so shocked that she fell to her knees sobbing. "This man did not lay a finger on her at all, instead she pushed him", Ms. Hopkins said to the officer, she continue to say," the child is staying here with her father"

Tina couldn't take what she was hearing anymore, she squeezed the knife even tighter, Destiny just stood next to her confused about why she was crying. Then Tina stood up and said "I'm taking my fucking baby outta here and you can't stop me" with rage in her voice. Destiny jumped and screamed, Tina then revealed the knife and pulled Destiny close to her. "I'm leaving this house with my baby" she said again. When Tavon saw what Tina had in her hand he went into shock and Ms. Hopkins screamed out "O my God she has a knife" Tina then proceeded to the living room holding Destiny by the hand. Both of the officers pulled out

Ebony Chronicles of Elevation

their guns, "Put the knife down ma'am... now" one of the officers said with authority. Tina just stood there shaking with the knife in her hand; she didn't know what she was going to do at this point. When Destiny saw the police pull out their guns she screamed again and said "mommy, mommy" Tina looked down at her and said "don't worry baby I won't let them take you". One of the officers moved in closer, Tina backed up towards the living room window. "Lady please put the knife down, you don't want to do this" the officer said. Tina had no more room to move, she was in the corner and out of options. She looked out the window and saw more police cars had pulled up outside and those officers were on their way up to the apartment. She then told the officer to back off or else. He then replied and told her to let the baby go or he was going to shoot. When the officer said that, Tina became scared. More police officers came in. Tavon and Ms. Hopkins just stood there in the living watching in disbelief to see what was going to happen next. As more officers entered the apartment Tina became overwhelmed and realized it was a hostage situation now, there were more guns and a taser pointed at her.

After about a half an hour of talking to the officers, Tina decided to release Destiny but as soon as she did that she put the knife to her own throat. One of the officers gave Destiny to Tavon and they left the apartment until the situation was resolved. Ms. Hopkins left as well. As they entered the hall way of the apartment to wait outside there was a loud gunshot noise and scream. Tavon's stomach dropped, he couldn't believe what he just heard. Destiny heard the noise also and hugged Tavon's neck tighter. When they walked outside, the entire parking lot was full of police cars, barricades and an ambulance. Almost every neighbor was looking out of their window. Tavon felt embarrassed, but all he cared about was the safety of his "heart" and that was Destiny. The paramedics went into the building, Tavon continued to hold Destiny in his arms and waited to see if Tina was dead, "I hope they didn't kill the poor girl" Ms. Hopkins said, Tavon didn't reply he just thought to himself ,why is all this happening.

Once again felt like he just couldn't catch a break, and the more he kept a positive attitude and was positive to others the more things didn't work out. Ms. Hopkins then said "Tavon don't worry things happen for a reason and God has a plan for everyone, it's going to get better" Tavon looked up in shock and in confusion; he didn't realize he was thinking out loud. "Thanks Ms. Hopkins" he said. An officer dressed in plain clothes came over and told them what happened inside of the apartment. Tina did get shot but she just wounded and they are about to bring her down. Within five minutes of standing with Destiny in his arms and talking to Ms. Hopkins the paramedics brought Tina out on a stretcher, her eyes were close and she had a bandage on her shoulder. Tavon still couldn't believe that Tina got shot but after seeing Tina act like that, he was just glad Destiny was ok. He was glad that Destiny was asleep when they brought Tina out, because he did not want her to see her mother like that.

After everything cleared out and Ms. Hopkins left, Tavon and Destiny went back towards the apartment, by that time Amber had arrived and the neighborhood was at peace again. As Amber was holding Destiny, Tavon heard his phone ringing, he ran upstairs to see who it was. He didn't recognize the number but he answered it anyway,. "I'm trying to get in contact with Tavon Coats," the man on the phone said. "Yes this is Tavon," he replied. The man on the phone said that he was with BBC construction, Tavon's eyes opened wide, it was the manager's position he applied for. The guy on the phone told Tavon that they were impressed with his resume and that they wanted to hire him as soon as possible.

Ebony Chronicles of Elevation

This was the best news Tavon had heard all week, because this was the job that he originally wanted. After he finished talking to the guy on the phone about the job he sat on the couch, with the phone still in his hand, at this point Tavon was so happy and fulfilled, he felt like all of the struggles with Tina and financial issues was finally over. He always dreamed about this moment, but now it was upon him. Tavon took a deep breath in and out and started to relax, then his phone started to ring, it was the dogs barking ringtone again, his heart dropped "O' hell no" he yelled out, then Amber started to laugh out loud, he looked up and saw Amber had Tina's phone, then both of them started to laugh out loud.

Willow Brook

Norris Pimpton

Prologue

When I was twelve years old I saw my mother shoot my father dead. Right between his eyes the bullet flew through skin, then bone, then through flashes of his life until the lights went completely out. I thought it was maybe an accident then. I thought that my mother meant to scare him as he raised his hand to tattoo another knuckle print on the side of her face. I thought she didn't mean it as she held the stub nose six chamber beast by the handle with both hands shaking. I thought he would back off and leave her alone but he didn't. He lowered his hand, looked down at me and laughed. I will never forget that laugh. Laughing like Richard Pryor was in our living room giving him his own personal show. But the only thing on the stage that night was metal filled with six shells of death. Then just like it started, the laughter stopped, and the smile his eyes held turned into piercing rays of heat burning my chest. "Deion go to your room" my father said to me in a deep dark tone as calm and as smooth as I've ever heard it.

I couldn't move, my feet were glued to the floor and my eyes were glued to that gun. He turned back toward my mother and did what I hadn't expected. He moved toward her one pointy toed brown dress shoe after the other. He took short easy strides seeming to dare her to pull the hammer back and ring death into him. At first I thought it was a mistake when I heard the click of the gun being pulled back by her thumb. My head snatched up and I looked into my mother's eyes. Her Redding eyes squinted and her front teeth bit down on her bottom lip and showed me an expression I've never seen before that night. I heard the sound of his soles meeting linoleum stop.

"Bitch you better put down that gun before I kill you where you stand"

I stood there watching his forehead wrinkle into madness. I looked down at his hand and he was wiggling his fingers like they did in the old western movies before a gun fight. The only difference is the only one holding the gun in the room was my mother. In that moment my heart could have crashed through my rib cage. In that moment I thought he would stop when she refused to put down the gun. I figured that he would grab his coat and hat and head out the door. Instead he lunged toward her with his left arm raised up toward the ceiling then down on brown flesh with a smack that echoed through the living room. I looked up at my mother again, and she held her hand over bruised flesh and tears. My heart was jumping around my chest trying to break free, trying to run away from what was coming next. He reached with his right hand for the gun but before he had a chance to grab it my mother raised it back up at his chest.

-BANG-BANG-BANG-BANG-.

The sound of metal meeting flesh, meeting death echoed throughout our house until he was nothing but a heap of flesh stuck to the cold living room floor. My mother dropped the gun, looked down at my daddy's lifeless body and scream. She screamed, held her head in her hands and dropped down to her knees yelling "No" over and over again. And still I couldn't move.

Five years later:

The pavement down 118th St. was hot today. The heat rose up from concrete side walk and seeped though the rubber of my Chuck Taylor's. I wore tan khakis, a white tee shirt and a tan hat tilted down just over my eyes. I had half a Key in a black back pack slung over my right shoulder, so I was in a hurry to dump this off and get back to my stash and make another drop. I preferred to walk if the drop was this close in case one time decided to flip his lights on for driving while black. No Id. No drives license I would have been sent up for sure. I wasn't going to jail today or any other day if I could help it. I thought about the letter I got from my mother yesterday that told me that she will be coming home soon. The date on the letter and the date she told me was only three days away. With that, I imagined what she would be like after five years in prison, wondered if she still had that same smile that lit up the room. Something inside told me she couldn't, something told me that those cold concrete walls robbed it from her as she slept. The fact that my daddy was dead and she was behind bars robbed me of mine. I held no animosity against my mother, I felt as I grew up that she had no other choice. I remember seeing her time and time again get knocked upside her head for things I didn't understand. So I made peace with it the best way that I could.

After the shooting I had a choice to either go live with my cousin Tommy and my Auntie Val around the corner from my house on Antwerp a few houses down from 120th, or to Long Beach with my Auntie Jeanette. I loved Jeanette but I chose to stay closer to what was familiar, so Antwerp is where I went. I had to survive out here the best way I knew how. So I took up the occupation of my peers, the only occupation I know would keep the cramps of missed meals as far away from me as possible. I'd received other letters from my mother telling me how she missed me and

169

Ebony Chronicles of Elevation

was looking forward to getting out. She always apologized for being away from me for as longs as she was, but what choice did she have. I allowed too many painful thoughts to dance around in my mind; all I wanted to do was forget. My mother told me she was going to make things right when she came home. Also, that she wanted me to make better choices then what she had made. In all the letters she would always tell me that everyone has a choice no matter how the situation looks. I thought about that, then I looked out at my surroundings and it was hard to see. I didn't see any other choice then what I was doing now, even though in the pit of my stomach I knew this wasn't right. In the many letters she wrote to me I expected that she would say something about my father but she never did. Maybe she didn't want me to re-live the memory of his murder. Maybe she was trying to block it out herself. What she didn't know is that those images often crept in while I slept. What she wouldn't expect is that I've change from the little boy she knew. These concrete streets filled with horrors a child shouldn't see, embedded in my psyche like a parasite. I was not the same scared little boy that wanted the lights kept on at night. Now I preferred the cover of darkness. These streets were forced upon me and the once feared blocks of concrete, became my shelter. I was becoming something else, something that looked forward to the miscommunication and mayhem of those streets. Drug dealers and pimps became my comrades and dope fiends became my way to easy wealth. I felt like a vampire in that the darkness was my salvation, and as the dark shadows hit the uneven blocks between Imperial and 120th, so did the people with money in outstretched hands. Yearning for that feel good hit that would take them to heaven, if just for a little while. I thought that I'd be a fool to pass that up only to starve and be draped in hand me down cloths. In the mist of my madness I thought about how my mother would look at me, and that thought made me uneasy. I promised myself that I would only do this until she came home. I already had enough money stacked up to last for a good while but I was going to make as much as I could with the few days I had left.

I would read my mother's letters then stare at the words and wondered how she expected me to be when she got out. Everyone around me hustled in one form or another. If they weren't scamming the system, using relatives to get more food stamps or slagging these white rocks of death. Then they were dead or in prison, so my only teachers were what were around me. Either I was going to be a victim or I was going to be a survivor. So I chose to do what was needed, right or wrong. I was doing the only thing I knew how to do to survive on these streets. In my mind, at the moment I thought I didn't have a choice. I wanted to make sure we had enough money put up to take care of us or die trying. With my daddy gone I knew it was going to be hard on her, so I would do this until she came home.

I understand how swiftly death could show up but I was never afraid for my safety. After seeing my daddy killed in front of me, nothing shook me. I understood more about death then someone my age should know. I thought back about my cousin Corn Bread, he died a few years before my father was killed. I remember with clarity one of the last times I saw him. I got out of our 1977 gray Volkswagen, put my white Pro wings on the concrete streets of Willow book Ave in Compton. Before I reached to open my grandmother's gate I noticed a weaving shopping cart full of cans moving up the block towards us. One arm bent under the handle, right leg moving uneasily toward some unknown destination. My mother moved in front of me, opened the gate, walked under the huge palm tree that hung like a guardian over the house and went up to knock on the door. We waited for a few seconds as my grandfather opened the door to let us in.

"Hey baby."

My grandmother said as we walked through the door stamping wet kisses on my forehead. I followed a sweet smell to the kitchen where she kept all kinds of cakes and pies. The kitchen was small with a little round table set next to an old refrigerator in front of the window. Corn Bread sat there with a green cup and a bottle half way full with brown liquid.

"What's up Deion?"

He slurred out in a voice like Woody the wino from Sanford and Son.

Corn bread was always drunk or getting drunk every time we saw him. He would tell us slurred stories of things and places we never understood. But we laughed and talked along with him anyway. Up to that point we never saw his sober side and as far as we knew his veins always flowed with alcohol.

I thought about him because the week he finally became sober he walked up in the middle of a squabble between a couples next door to my grandmother's house. He walked up with the intent to help someone solve a problem, unfortunately just like his was about to be. The only problem was that the man that he was trying to stop; knock lumps upside his girlfriend head and didn't care that he was a week from being so drunk that he couldn't say his name clear enough nor could he understand it. He didn't care because at that moment he couldn't see through his rage. And as he pulled a black Beretta from the small of his back, there was no time for my cousin to do anything else but die.

I crossed Success from East 118th St. to Carver Park, walked through the parking lot, past the play ground to the back fence near the elementary. Curtis was supposed to meet me here at 5:00 but he wasn't there. I glanced back at the school and remembered how I use to walk those halls, how I use to sit in the lunch room and watch the cafeteria workers with their black hair nets dance behind the counter. How I loved to be in Ms. Petersons class because she help to turn my worst subject into my favorite. She took her time to make sure that light went off in my head, and the brightness of my eyes let her know that I finally understood what I was doing. I saw myself on that playground and I remembered back then how different I saw the world. I thought that I could do anything, be in any position I wanted to be. For a second I willed myself back to that time. Thought about my mother and how she would walk me across the street to school every morning. This park held too many memories of a far different time. Even though there was things going on around me that I wasn't aware of until know. My mother kept me from its evils until they took her away. I'm sure she'll be disappointed that the things she tried to shield me from, I have become. So I continued to stare at my yesterdays' as I stood in the present, a fragment of what I was. I wasn't sure if that little boy was in there anymore. No matter how much I tried to get in touch with him I couldn't. All I could do now was wish that things could have been different. Thought that maybe I could have changed something if I had another chance to talk to my father. Maybe I could have found a way to show him that we needed him to show us more than rage and hate. He might have figured that our lives were worth more than his intoxicated states of sadness. Wished I had a chance to spend more time with him. All I could do was wish I had times with him when he wasn't drunk and angry at the world for his faults. I wished that I had a normal family that was not surrounded in so much pain. I understood my reality as I stood there staring at what I used to be, thinking of things that I couldn't change and I

Ebony Chronicles of Elevation

knew that it was too late for all that. What was done was done and nothing I could have done to turn that clock back. Nothing.

I eased my hand in my pocket, took my cell phone out. No text, no missed calls. Slide the phone back in my pocket and looked around and didn't see his six foot two frame bouncing toward me in any direction. I met Curtis a few weeks after I moved in with my Auntie. He lived with his grandmother around the corner and with both his parents murdered by stray bullets we had some kind of connection. The only thing is Cutis never talked about them; I heard stories about them from his grandmother. How his daddy moved the family up from El Dorado, Arkansas for better work. He acted like they never existed. Times when I would bring them up he would stay quiet and look at me like he saw a ghost. So after awhile I stopped bringing it up. I look at the time on my phone again and wondered where he was. One thing he knew is that I didn't like waiting around for long in one place. If I was going to get caught up by the police or a jacker it was going to be on the move. So I knew either something happened or he got slowed down. Either way I wasn't waiting around to find out so I headed back the way I came. Back past the play ground toward the parking lot when a brown two tone coupe de Ville rolled through and stopped just before I stepped foot in the parking lot. All I saw was light skin and gold teeth beaming at me.

"What's up little Nigga"

I looked at him, my forehead wrinkled wanting to reach for the gun I normally carried but wasn't there. I looked down and a polished 357 Magnum gazed back at me and seemed to smile. My anger grew. I took off my hat and threw it at the car.

"Tom, what the hell I tell you about pointing guns at me fool!"

Norris Pimpton

All I heard was laughter filling the car, then spilling out as my cousin Tommy, Freddy and my homeboy Curtis leaped out laughing like three crazed hyenas.

"You fools better go somewhere before I fire on ya'll ass in your sleep."

They laughed even louder at that. I guess knowing I didn't like to play like that made it even funnier for them. I guessed that pretending they were going to shoot someone was somehow funny. Tommy handed me a brown cigarette filled with something he keeps telling me that would put my mind at ease, like I'm Craig of that movie *Friday*. I never tried it, and if it was going to have me acting as stupidly as he acted then I never would. So they all stood there puffing and passing it around like chiefs on a reservation deep in Oklahoma. I wanted to start walking back up 118th but against my better judgment I stayed and waited on them.

"Come on Deion there is some work off Willowbook let's go take care of this,"

Curtis said trying to bring me back to the reason why I was there in the first place.

"What's up? I thought we were doing this thing right here?"

"Yea but Keisha called and said she can't get this way, so we have to go where she is right now."

"Where she is? She knows the deal, either she come pick it up here or she don't need it that bad."

"That's what I told her homie, said she tried but she has no way to get this way, the money is waiting for us though."

There was nothing else that needed to be said, I picked my hat up off the ground slapped it against my leg a few times to knock off the dirt and got in the car. There was money to be made and at that time nothing else was more important then that. As we loaded back in the car there was a loud whistle coming from behind us. I turned back and a

Ebony Chronicles of Elevation

dope fiend we called Twin jogged up to the car smiling and pulling on a dirty wife beater that was too big for his body.

"What's up Deion man, you got anything?"

"What you looking for?"

"Give me a fifty piece."

I turned back toward Curtis and ask him to break him off a fifty I knew he had on him. Turned back to Twin and he couldn't stop pulling on his tee shirt, wiping and swatting his face. I stood there looking at Twin decay right in front of me and I did nothing. I knew all I had to do was tell him I was out and he would be gone like he was never there. But that money seemed to speak louder then my morals, so I stood there looking back at Curtis wishing he would hurry up. He soon jumped out the car handed him the rock wrapped in foil. Twin put the money in his hand and jogged off up Success toward Imperial. So we both looked at each other then around and got in the car and drove off.

We pulled out of the park down Success Ave. and east on 120th. The car stopped at the light on Compton Ave. next to a Shell gas station. Little kids and mothers with empty faces walked across in front of us just before the light changed. We made a right on Wilmington, down 124th and stopped right before Willowbrook Ave.

"You got the strip with you?"

I asked Curtis before I stepped one foot to the pavement.

"Hell yea I got the strip, you know I don't leave home without it. We don't need it anyway fool, we been dealing with Keisha for a minute.

"Get your scary ass out the car and go make that money," Freddy said from the driver's seat, looking at me through the rear view mirror.

My forehead wrinkled and I opened my mouth to say something but instead I opened the car door to get out.

I climbed out and walked toward the house with Curtis behind me. A black bared screen door swung open as we neared the door and we stopped and watched who came out.

"Come on through the back yard, my daddy on the couch sleep and I don't want his grumpy ass to wake up," Keisha told us as she came out and rounded the corner leading us to the back of the house. We knew the drill; get in there, get our money and get out of there. No bullshittin around, make the exchange and keep it moving. We all knew better. Even though we knew Keisha, we didn't know the house and who might have been inside. And for some reason we didn't question it, we just went to the back without a thought. Walked in the back door to nothing but a card table with a black bag on top, a TV sitting on top of a milk crate and a young dude whose hand is attached to a remote control playing Madden with no sound on Play Station. There was a dim light that hung above the table but it wasn't enough light to illuminate the whole room. It was hard to tell where the other walls were.

"Keisha, why you got us in this dark ass room? Turn some more lights on around here so we can see what we doing."

Curtis said as he took his hat turning it around backward maybe trying to see clearer.

"Did you bring the stuff?"

Is all she said as she giggled and patted her hand on the table so that I could place it there. I figured she laughed because of the paranoia in Curtis's voice, so I slid the bag off my shoulder and headed toward the table.

"Hold up Deion, where is the money Keisha?"

She looked at me then at Curtis and smiled, and then her smiled turned to laughter. I hadn't noticed that

Ebony Chronicles of Elevation

the image on the TV screen stopped moving. The quiet dude on the couch was now standing. I turned back toward Curtis and he was still arguing with Keisha.

"What you think this is fool?"

She pointed down at the bag sitting on the table. She motion for me to bring the back pack and sit it down next to it.

"What the fuck is that!?"

Is the last thing I heard Curtis say as I heard the click of a door knob and the lights go out. In the next few seconds there was scuffling of feet and then gun fire. I tried to turn back to the door we came in but I felt surging heat in the left side of my chest. I felt my finger tips tingle then I felt the blood run up and down both of my arms like water in an angry sea. I only saw flashes of light as more gun fire's deafening sound in that small room explode. I turned toward where I thought the door was and again I felt fire hit me twice in the back and I went down. A few more guns shots and the room fell silent; I thought explosions of the guns took my hearing away. Thought maybe I was dead and I fell into the pit of darkness that fast. I yelled out and my own voice echoed back at me. My hands started to feel rubbery and numb; my chest felt like it was on fire. I yelled out to Curtis and heard nothing, not sound, no breathing, nothing. I tried to push myself as far as I could back and against a wall so I could try and stand up. I finally managed to reach the wall and left myself to my feet. I couldn't see and didn't know what direction I was but I reached my hand out feeling along the wall for a door knob. All of a sudden a deep rattled cough broke the silence.

"Curtis!?"

No reply, just more coughing and then complete silence. So I continued to search the wall for a way out of here. I heard a familiar click and I froze, I wanted to yell out but I thought best not to. I wanted to run but I didn't know in what direction so I just stood where I was. Then just like I heard the click, the gun shot rang out and the bullet hit the wall along side me and I felt the wood fragments slitter on my face. In the stillness of that moment, instead of another click I heard a thud like something on a road runner cartoon. I stood still for a while, my breathing getting heavier and more labored but I stood still, afraid to move. I took one big breath that made my head spin so much that I almost hit the ground. I leaned into the wall and moved until I felt a door knob hitting me in the side. I grabbed the knob held it in my hand like a life jacket and I was in the middle of the sea. I took another breath and turned the knob and pulled and sunlight engulfed the room and stung my eyes. I took slow labored steps outside and around the corner to the side of the house. All I could hear was loud banging music coming from the car my cousins in. I looked at bobbing heads and hands passing smoke back and forth. Tommy turn and put his hand up and froze, he turn around to the driver side and got out. The last thing I heard was yelling seeming to get further and further away until I was engulfed in darkness.

I opened my eyes one at a time, the taste of funk danced around my mouth and I felt sick to my stomach. I lay there not knowing how long I was out, bullet fragments embedded deep in my flesh, but I was glad to be alive. I looked toward the curtains and a little sunlight reach through a small opening. I looked over at the other side of the bed for a button to call the nurse. At that moment I needed the sunlight in the room. I needed to feel something besides pain if only for a few seconds. So I pressed the button for the nurse and waited to feel something, to feel anything. I lay there and thought about how stupid it was to get mixed up in sick games like that. I thought about the shameful look on my mother's face if she could see me like this. Thought what she would say, thought that after

Ebony Chronicles of Elevation

having to deal with prison that she would turn and run at the sight of her half dead son.

I heard the door squeak open and I turned my head toward the sound as the nurse walked in.

"How are you feeling?"

"A lot of pain"

"Okay honey I'll get you something to ease it"

"Can you please open the curtain all the way up?"

She smiled and walked over and opened the curtain as far as they would go. The sunlight rushed in like a raging water fall and it felt good. I looked through the window as the nurse walked by, out the door and wondered if Curtis was in one of these rooms. All I could remember was bullets firing at us in the darkness. I heard no scream, no sound at all; so maybe he got away in time. Maybe he was at home sleep in his own bed dreaming about another place.

The door pushed opened again and I forced my body to turn back around so that I could take the pills the nurse had for me. I looked up at her face, her eyes, her hair braided up in some crazy style. She had a denim jacket over a white tee shirt with Obama's smiling picture on it. I looked back up at her face and a tear first out of her left eye then her right, fall like a slow mist. My heart felt like it exploded for real inside of my chest at that moment. I hadn't expected to see my mother here, didn't want her to see me laying here like this. I couldn't take the disappointment in her eyes, but as I looked at them, I saw none. All I saw was worry and concern splashed across her face. I opened my mouth to say something but I couldn't speak She seemed unable to move so she stood there, and I lay there frozen in awkwardness. Maybe wondering how we both got here, and as my own tears welled up in the corners of my eyes I felt overwhelming love radiating from her. I felt

that my savoir had come home and all the pain and worry
that lay on my shoulders would be finally at rest.

ABOUT THE CONTRIBUTORS

COREY J. BARNES is a long time native of Lakeland, Florida. Currently he resides there with his son Corey Jr. He holds a Bachelor's degree in Education from the University of South Florida by way of Tuskegee University (AL), a Master's degree in Educational Leadership from Saint Leo University (FL), and is currently working on his PhD in Instructional Leadership and Adult Education from Nova University (FL).

Becoming an published author and also establishing the publishing company Jaye Luv Publishing LLC has fulfilled a lifelong dream for Corey as he attempts to bring true romance and integrity back to urban fiction, from a male perspective, hence his moniker, "The Renaissance Man of Romance".

In his debut novel What Is This Love Thing All About? (2009) and follow up Single For The Night (2010), Corey displays that chivalry is not dead and the thrill of the chase is still present in today's world.

Presently, Corey is working on an anthology to be included in a book set for release in the spring of 2012. Corey is also beginning to work on a screenplay as well. In addition to his work as a high school administrator and college adjunct professor, Corey also coaches high school boys basketball and his son's little league football team. He serves on the board of directors with various youth groups in the Lakeland community and is actively involved in his fraternity, Kappa Alpha Psi Inc. When he is not writing, he enjoys spending time with his son, reading, exercising, and traveling.

CHRIS HICKS is an established author who runs his own publishing company in Baltimore, Maryland, Universal Publishing

Co LLC. He is the founder of the BUBF (BALTIMORE URBAN BOOK FESTIVAL). He has written his first book, THINK volume 1 which will be released this fall 2011. His book was written with young adult men in mind, with step by step advice on how to build stronger, positive and healthier family relationships.

Chris continues to be involved in nonprofit efforts and has served as well as donated to various charity organizations such as the House of Ruth and Play Kidz Learning Center. He is an active role model in the community, as well as a volunteer for Big Sister, Big Brother of Central Maryland. Chris, who describes himself as a classic overachiever, has garnered an impressive list of community involvement activities such as being a member of The Urban League Young Professionals who targets education and the youth in our communities.

MOSES MILLER is a journalist, a motivational speaker and an award winning author for Mind Candy, LLC, which is a company focused on book publishing, the development of screenplays and educational programming for our youth. A native New Yorker, Moses exhibits the uncanny ability to capture the pulse of the streets with intelligent and well thought out storylines. In the past, he has contributed articles and written for various websites and publications including The Voice, Newsday and 88HIPHOP.COMwhere he is currently the Editor in Chief of content. He holds a Bachelors degree in Business Management and a Master of Science degree in Technology Management obtained from Polytechnic University. His first novel, Nan: The Trifling Times of Nathan Jones has received various awards and critical acclaim from readers and book clubs around the world. After the successful release of his first novel, Mr. Miller cemented a deal with F.E.D.S. magazine resulting in a joint venture to publish his second release, Once Upon A Time in Harlem in September of 2007. The highly anticipated second installment in the Nan series, The Game of Trife, was released through Mind

Candy, LLC in August of 2008. Mr. Miller is a socially conscious individual who strives to play a key role in helping to improve the literacy rates amongst African American and Hispanic teens. Through his American Me "Voices of Our Youth" program, he has worked with several other organizations in an effort to decrease the high school dropout rates plaguing lower income communities. Mr. Miller's inspirational book The Barack in Me, was written specifically for young African American males, with themes that cross the boundaries of gender and race. Mr. Miller is currently the facilitator for two youth mentoring programs focused on developing upstanding men and community leaders. His latest release, Nan: The Trifecta is the highly anticipated finale to his Nan series.

OMAR TYREE, is a New York Times best-selling author, a journalist, reporter, poet, screenwriter, songwriter, playwrite, event host, lecturer, blogger, publishing consultant and literacy advocate, who has won a 2001 NAACP Image Award for Outstanding Literature in Fiction, a 2006 Phillis Wheatley Literary Award for Body of Work in Urban Fiction, and a 2010 HBCU Legends Award for his tiresome work in urban literacy.
Born and raised in Philadelphia, Pennsylvania, where he graduated from the prestigious Central High School in 1987, Tyree first attended the University of Pittsburgh as a Pharmacy major and an aspiring football player. After spending his first two years at Pitt, he found his new passion and a calling as a writer and a storyteller, penning his first published series, "The Diary of a Freshman" along with two novels; "Colored, On White Campus", (now titled "College Boy" in his Urban Griot series) and "Flyy Girl", which became a contemporary urban classic that spawned an entire genre of so-called "urban/street literature."

Tyree transferred to the respected HBCU of Howard University to finish his education as a writer in the Fall of 1989. Leaving the English Department in the School of the Liberal Arts for the School of Communications, he graduated cum laude with a degree in Print Journalism in the fall of 1991. While at Howard, he created, produced and published "Food For Thought" a student opinion column in "The Hilltop" newspaper, along with publishing several Washington, DC-based news articles for the Black Press.

Upon graduation from Howard, Tyree established his own publishing company, MARS Productions, in early 1992, at the tender age of 23. He then self-published and marketed his first three novels, including "Capital City", which chronicled Washington, DC's violent drug culture, and went on to sell 25,000 copies of his first three titles with distribution sources from Newport News, Virginia, to Queens, New York.

By the Spring of 1995, Tyree's activity had attracted the attention of several major publishing houses, including Simon & Schuster, where he signed his first two-book publishing deal for a six-figure advance payment at age 26.

And as they say, the rest is his-story. Tyree went on to publish 16 novels, two short story books, and one non-fiction book on "The Equation" of entrepreneurship and business. To date, he has sold more than 2 million copies of his books worldwide, and has created a brand name in the publishing industry that has generated more than $30 million.

Tyree has also been published in five anthology books, several major newspapers, including; The Washington Post, The Philadelphia Inquirer, and The News Journal; several national magazines, including, Ebony, Essence, Upscale, The Black Collegian, and The Washington View, and featured on the national blog web site TheDailyVoice.com.

Along with his many literary awards from various national organizations, Tyree has founded and formed his own nonprofit arm of the Urban Literacy Project (ULP), where he highlights "The 5 Key Components of Literacy" (Reading, Writing, Thinking, Visualization and Application). Penning a short short book, "12 Brown Boys" for young urban readers in September of 2008, Tyree was cited by the City Council of Philadelphia for his tireless community work in urban literacy in the Spring of 2009, where he spoke about the need to continue the fight against illiteracy within the urban American community.

Hailed as one of the most passionate and informed speakers on artistic, community, educational, cultural, intellectual, popular and business topics, Tyree has been a featured lecturer at more than 50 major American institutions, colleges and universities, including Harvard and Yale.

For more information on his career work and various titles, please view his web site @ www.OmarTyree.com.

NORRIS PIMPTON is a native of Los Angeles, CA. Currently he resides in Dallas Texas. His lifelong dream of becoming an published author has been fulfilled. His debut novel The Project Diaries (2010) and his anticipated novel Hotel 23 (2012), will be released soon.

Norris is also working on a stage play called Echoes in the Dark, and will be followed up with more plays and novels. When Norris is not writing he enjoys reading and traveling.

Q.B. WELLS is the publisher of Art Official Media LLC and an author living in Baltimore City, Maryland. He has written books (*Blackface*, *Doughboy*), book reviews, articles and essays about urban literature and culture for *The Urban Book Source*, *Urbania Magazine* and www.UrbaniaMag.com. A member of the Independent Book Publishers Association, Q.B. Wells presents workshops on publishing at local community centers and organizations.

A visionary and entrepreneur, Q.B. Wells taught with the Baltimore City Public School System for several years before transitioning into teaching writing classes at Towson University. *One Hundred Miles and Running* (Blackface 2) is his second novel.

EYONE WILLIAMS was born and raised in Washington, D.C. He is a publisher, author, rapper and actor representing urban life in a way that is uniquely his. Known for hard-core, gritty novels. Eyone made the Don Diva best-seller list with his first novel, Fast Lane (Fast Lane Publications). He followed up his debut novel with Hell Razor Honeys 1 and 2 (Cartel Publications). He then delivered his readers a short story entitled The Cross (DC Bookdiva Publications). He's also a staff writer for Don Diva Magazine, his most notable work is featured in Don Diva's issue 30, *The Good, The Bad, and The Ugly,* where he outlined the rise and fall of D.C. street legends Michael "Fray" Salters and Wayne Perry.

Eyone's first acting role was in the forthcoming movie *Dark City* (District Hustle). His latest mixtape, *A Killer'z Ambition,* is a sound track to the novel, A Killer'z Ambition (DC Bookdiva Publications) by Nathan Welch. His latest novel, Lorton Legends (DC Bookdiva Publications), is one of the most acclaimed books of the present day. For more information about Eyone Williams visit his Facebook page: facebook.com/eyone.williams; also follow him on Twitter @eyonethewriter.

Other Titles from NCM Publishing:

Over and Over Again
The Appetizer, When You're Not His Main Course
Strawberries, Stilettos, and Steam
Twisted
Mama Don't Like Ugly
My Mama's Sweet Potato Pie/
El Pay de Camote de mi Mama
The Twins
A Little Sumthin' Sumthin'
Voices of Cyn…Traces of a Backslider
A Cold Piece
Miles Apart
Ebony Chronicles of Elevation
Whispers of Words Spoken
When is Strong Strong Enough?
A Generation of Curses
Are There French Fries in Heaven?
Lil' Creepers Winter Shenanigans

For any questions or comments
Please email us at
info@ncmpublishing.com

Also,
Follow us on twitter
@ncmpublishing

NCM Publishing 2012 Releases

Made in the USA
Charleston, SC
01 May 2012